THE BLACKGAARD CHRONICLES™

BOOK ONE
OPENING MOVES

THE BLACKGAARD CHRONICLES™

BOOK ONE
OPENING MOVES

PHIL LOLLAR

The Blackgaard Chronicles: *Opening Moves*
© 2017 Focus on the Family. All rights reserved.

Focus on the Family and Adventures in Odyssey, and the accompanying
logos and designs, are federally registered trademarks of Focus on the
Family, 8605 Explorer Drive, Colorado Springs, CO 80920.

This book is based on Adventures in Odyssey audio drama episodes
"Connie, Part 1" and "Connie, Part 2"; "An Encounter with Mrs.
Hooper"; "A Bite of Applesauce"—original script by Paul McCusker;
"Connie Comes to Town"—original script by Steve Harris and Phil Lollar;
and "Recollections"—original script by Phil Lollar.

Novelization by Phil Lollar

Cover design by Jacob Isom
Cover illustration by Gary Locke

For Library of Congress Cataloging-in-Publication Data for this title,
visit http://www.loc.gov/help/contact-general.html.

ISBN: 9-781-58997-926-0

Printed in the United States of America
23   22   21   20   19   18   17
7   6   5   4   3   2   1

For Katie Leigh

CHAPTER ONE

P hilip Glossman was hungry. He had missed lunch that afternoon because of an Odyssey City Council meeting, and now it was past his suppertime. His potbelly rumbled, and he felt weak, but he knew he couldn't leave. Not yet. Not until *he* called. The note said *he* would, sometime this evening. *He* didn't like to leave messages, and *he* certainly wouldn't like it if *his* phone call weren't answered because of something so mundane as eating. So supper would have to wait.

He hadn't called in almost five years, just communicated through occasional written messages, mainly commenting on Glossman's monthly reports, or telling him what issues to raise and how to vote on them. If *he* wanted to actually talk this time, something important must be brewing—something very important.

Glossman paced the length of his top-floor office in the McAlister building, stopped in front of a small mirror hanging on the wall opposite his desk, and stared into it. *I need to get outside more,* he thought. *My skin is getting pasty.* He ran his fingers through his thinning salt-and-pepper hair and counted the lines around his gray eyes.

I used to be better looking, he mused. Not that he was bad now, just not like when he first came to town. Now he'd grown soft, mushy, out of shape.

He sighed. How did he wind up in a podunk village like Odyssey? He'd been a rising star in the New York City business scene, a smart, ruthless go-getter.

A bit too much of a go-getter, as it turned out. He thought he had covered all of the bases—that no one would ever know about how he manipulated that deal. But what was the verse those Bible thumpers Whittaker and Riley were always quoting? "Be sure your sin will find you out."

Well, he was found out all right, but not by his sin. By *him*. *He* discovered everything somehow, and *he* gave Glossman a choice: go to prison or go to Odyssey. So now *he* was calling the shots—and not calling on the phone—just to show who was in charge.

Glossman's belly rumbled louder. He turned away from the mirror and looked at the phone. "Why don't you *ring* already!" he muttered. But the phone just sat there, silently defiant.

Glossman moved to the window. There was hardly any traffic on the streets. Everyone was heading home. Everyone but him. He sighed again. He didn't have it bad, really, with the exception of tonight. His benefactor paid him well, albeit under the table. He was a respected member of the tiny community, all but permanently seated on its highest governing body. And all he had to do for the money and the position was prepare the monthly reports that pretty much detailed what Whittaker and Riley were up to, which, since their last big run-in, was mostly Whittaker working late and Riley doing nothing.

His thoughts turned bitter. Whittaker and Riley. Two names he'd love to never hear again, belonging to two people he'd love to never hear *from* again. They were the real reason he was still stuck in Odyssey. They'd outmaneuvered him, wrecking things, thwarting plans, keeping *him* in check, though neither of them realized that's what they were doing.

Glossman had failed and was still being punished for it. Instead of wheeling and dealing on Wall Street, he was now wheedling and dealing on the Odyssey City Council over things like easements and red zones and beautification projects. And his opponent on almost every single issue was Tom Riley. Their battles were growing quite tiresome. The one they had today was the reason Glossman had missed lunch. How that apple-growing hick ever got elected to the council in the first place—much less elected chairman of the council—was a mystery. Or maybe not, now that Glossman thought about it. Riley's farm was one of the largest in the area, which gave him a lot of clout with the other farmers. They considered him a classic man of the people, no doubt. Glossman sneered. More like the champion yokel of the yokels.

Then there was Riley's friend Whittaker. John Avery Whittaker, do-gooding crusader, everybody's favorite, loved by kids and parents throughout Campbell County—and all because of that silly business of his: Whit's End. A piece of property that valuable, and Whittaker turned it into—how did he describe it?—a *discovery emporium*?

Glossman snorted. It was more like a playground with train sets and talking mirrors. Games and puzzles and gizmos. Ice-cream sundaes at the soda fountain. An "Inventors' Corner," where the kiddies could do little science projects, and a "Bible Room," where they could all learn to be do-gooders just like Whittaker and Riley. The snort nearly turned into a gag.

Whittaker couldn't possibly be making any money out of the place. Then again, being a rich man, he didn't have to, did he? That came as a surprise. He'd thought Whittaker was just a middle-school teacher. The city council had given him an award for excellence in education just prior to Glossman's election to the council. Taking that building should have been as easy as pie. Everything was going so well. Then Whittaker showed up.

No. Not Whittaker. *Mrs.* Whittaker. His wife, Jenny. She was the one who'd made things difficult. Glossman winced at the memory. He could still see her fiery red hair flying and her hazel eyes snapping and hear her whiny voice as it yammered away at them from the speaker's lectern, her husband watching from the audience and Riley sitting in the chairman's seat, listening with a smug smile on his face.

CHAPTER TWO

Five years earlier . . .

"The Fillmore Recreation Center was refurbished in 1934 as part of a Depression relief effort. It was designed to give families, especially youngsters, a place to engage in wholesome activities—such as sporting events and games—as well as serving as a public meeting place. Several churches and civic groups have made use of the facility throughout the years. In fact, the city council called the rec center home prior to this present location being built. It holds many treasured memories for the people of this town. And that alone should make it worth saving."

Riley's chair creaked as he leaned forward. "Well, thank you very much, Mrs. Whittaker. Does anyone on the council have any questions for Mrs. Whittaker about the rec center?"

"I do, Chairman Riley."

"I thought you might, Mr. Glossman."

"Mrs. Whittaker, it's obvious you've done your homework, and you are to be congratulated for your efforts. Tell me, in your research, did you find it to be the oldest building in town?"

Jenny brushed a strand of silver-red hair from her eyes, adjusted her glasses, and, looking uncomfortable, shifted her petite frame from one foot to the other. "Well, no, sir."

"Did you find it to be *one* of the oldest?"

"No, I didn't."

"As a matter of fact, there are several buildings older than Fillmore Center, aren't there?"

Jenny shifted again and placed her hands on the speaker's lectern, her hazel eyes glaring at Glossman. "Well, yes."

"So the center has no *real* historical value, does it, Mrs. Whittaker?"

"Only to the countless families who have used it over the past five decades, Mr. Glossman."

"Yes, well, I suppose that sentimental value is worth something. But as a piece of *true* history, the building is, in fact, quite worthless, correct?"

Jenny gripped the lectern. "Yes, as a piece of *true* history."

"Thank you, Mrs. Whittaker. That's all I have for now, Chairman Riley."

It was all Glossman could do to keep from smirking. *This is in the bag,* he thought. *She has nothing, and the only other witness is that doltish police cadet. Here he comes now. What's his name? Hardy? Harvey?*

"Officer David Harley, at your service! Although I'm really not an officer yet. I'm just a cadet, but soon I will be an officer—at least I hope. I'm waiting on the results of the written exam. There are more codes on the books in this town than you can shake a stick at. Which is not one of the codes, by the way, unless you're shaking a stick in a threatening manner, and you definitely don't want to be doing that. Especially if you're spitting on the sidewalk. I was just trying the *officer* label on for size, but technically, I'm Cadet David Harley, and I'm still at your service."

Glossman saw Jenny Whittaker sigh heavily and her husband stifle a giggle. *In the bag,* he thought.

Cadet Harley droned on incoherently for the next twenty minutes, and Glossman noticed the rest of the council, even Riley, barely staying awake, and Jenny sinking lower and lower in her seat. Finally the bumbling cadet uttered the words "So, in conclusion . . . ," and everyone in the room jerked awake.

Harley cleared his throat, then continued. "I think you'll agree that the biggest single cause of juvenile delinquency in this country today is young people. Now, I realize that may sound like a generalization, but if you were to take a look at a cross-section of all JDs"—he leaned toward the council—"that's police lingo for juvenile delinquents, by the way"—he leaned back again—"you'd probably find that most of them are between five and nineteen years of age. Coincidence? Maybe. But do we really want to take that chance? I don't think so." Cadet Harley nodded officially, then collected and stacked his papers on the lectern.

Tom Riley suppressed a smile. "Well, thank you for that enlightening testimony. Any questions from the council members? Mr. Glossman?"

"Yes. Cadet Harley, if I understand you correctly, you feel the Fillmore Recreation Center should be kept open in an effort to ward off juvenile delinquency?"

Harley nodded again. "Exactly."

"I didn't know we *had* a delinquency problem here in Odyssey."

Cadet Harley sniffed. "Councilman Glossman, I

myself have been a firsthand victim of juvenile delinquency. In fact, it was one of the reasons I decided to
go into law enforcement."

"Really?"

Harley took a small notepad from his shirt pocket
and consulted it. "The perpetrator was one Michael,
alias Mickey, Terrelli. He robbed me and then tried to
run away. So I apprehended him and made a citizen's
arrest."

"You actually ran after him and stopped him?"

"I had to. It was the only way I could get my pencil
box back."

"Your pencil . . . Cadet Harley, how old were you
when this so-called crime took place?"

The cadet's brow wrinkled. "Um, eight, I think."

"So what you're saying is that you personally have
had no real problems with the young people in this city
since you were eight years old?"

Cadet Harley blinked. Several times. "Well, of
course, it all depends on your perspective, but as far as

wrong goes, then, well, I'd have to say, yes, you're right. But . . ."

Riley cut in quickly. "Uh, I think that'll be all for now, Cadet Harley."

Harley blinked again. "Oh, okay." He gathered his papers and returned to his seat.

This is the moment, thought Glossman. *Time to take the prize.* "Chairman Riley, I'd like to make a motion that we dispense with the rest of these hearings. There is obviously not enough evidence to warrant keeping the old building."

"Now wait a minute!" Jenny Whittaker stormed up to the lectern. "Not enough evidence? What do you call all these people who just testified before you?"

"Mrs. Whittaker, we can see that you've garnered a great deal of support for your cause, but support and evidence are very different things. You yourself told us the building has no significant historical or cultural value, so we really can't justify making it a landmark. And Cadet Harley has just shown us that Odyssey has no real problems with its young people. So the idea that we should keep the Fillmore Recreation Center in an effort to ward off a sudden wave of juvenile delinquency is really rather absurd, don't you think?"

Jenny again gripped the lectern. "Has it ever occurred to you that the reason we haven't had problems in the past with our youth is precisely because of places like the Fillmore Recreation Center? Gentlemen, there is a tremendous amount of pressure on children, even the children of Odyssey, to grow up too fast. They need a place where they can be children. The Fillmore Center has been that place in the past, and with some renovation, it can be that place again."

"And how do you propose to pay for the renovations?" Glossman asked. "By using tax revenue, a move that will cost this city thousands of dollars? Now, I have before me a letter from the Webster Development Firm making us a very nice offer for the building and the land."

Jenny scoffed. "Yes, I've heard of the Webster Development Firm. They build minimalls."

"They're going to build a nice shopping center *with* facilities for children."

"Do you know what those so-called *facilities* will be, Mr. Glossman? A video-game arcade. The rest will be fast-food and party-supply stores. Nothing to help kids think and learn."

"That's your opinion, Mrs. Whittaker. But the fact is, the shopping center will provide revenue for the city instead of taking revenue from it."

Jenny gripped the lectern so tightly, her knuckles turned white. "Gentlemen, *please* don't do this! Don't let our children grow up in an atmosphere . . . that doesn't care what they do . . . or believe." Her face suddenly went very pale. She took a deep breath. "Please . . . don't . . . let this . . . happen."

She stopped again and hovered over the lectern. Mr. Whittaker stood up slowly. Riley frowned and leaned forward in his creaky chair. "Mrs. Whittaker? Mrs. Whittaker, are you all right?"

Jenny swayed slightly. "I'm . . . not feeling . . . very well." She moaned softly and, with great effort, turned to find her husband. Their eyes met, and she said weakly, "Whit?" Then her head slumped forward, and she collapsed on the floor.

The other council members gasped. Riley and Cadet Harley jumped from their chairs.

Whittaker was already out of his and rushed to her side. "Jenny? Jenny!" He lifted her gently and cradled her in his arms. "Jenny." He looked up help-lessly. "An ambulance! David! Tom! Somebody call an ambulance!"

✦

Word came later that evening that Jenny Whittaker had died. She had chronic kidney disease brought on by a bout of strep throat. By the time she collapsed, there was nothing the doctors could do. Whit was devastated. It was a shocking turn of events, but one Glossman fully intended to take advantage of.

A month passed. Out of respect for Jenny, the

council delayed any further discussion of the Fillmore Recreation Center, but Glossman knew as he took his seat in the council chamber the evening of the vote that it would be just a formality. His main opposition was out of the way—tragically, yes, but such was life. *Only a miracle can stop the sale now,* he thought, smiling. *That will make* him *very happy.*

Glossman sat patiently through the rest of the dreary business before the council. Finally the issue was at hand. Riley banged his gavel, and the council members quieted.

"On the matter of Mr. Glossman's motion to sell the Fillmore Recreation Center building, how does the council vote? Mr. Finster?"

"Aye."

"Mr. Calhoun?"

"Aye."

"Mr. Glossman?"

"Aye."

"And the chair votes nay." Riley sighed. "Mr.

Glossman, it looks like your motion is carried." He banged his gavel again.

"Thank you, Chairman Riley. I'd now like to propose that we follow through on this motion and immediately accept the generous offer the Webster Development Firm has made for the land and the building."

Finster raised his hand. "Second the motion."

Riley banged the gavel a third time. "The motion has been made and seconded. And since there are no other bidders on the property, I will suspend debate and call for a vote."

He was going to win!

"All in favor of the motion—"

The chamber doors burst open—and in strode Whittaker. "Mr. Chairman! May I address the council?"

Riley glanced around and said, "Well, we were just about to take a vote, Mr. Whittaker."

"If the vote concerns the Fillmore Recreation Center, that's what I'd like to talk about."

Alarm! Speak up! "Mr. Chairman, we've had enough grandstanding on this issue. My motion was made and seconded. You said there are no other bidders—"

"Oh, but there *is* another bidder," said Whittaker.

This couldn't be happening. The other council members were murmuring. Why were they murmuring? *You have to regain control. Say something.* "Mr. Whittaker," Glossman cut in, "is this some kind of joke?"

"Not at all, Mr. Glossman." Whittaker opened his briefcase and took out a stack of legal documents. He sidestepped the lectern, walked up to the council bench, and handed each member a copy of the documents. "I represent the Universal Press Foundation of Chicago. Their board of directors has instructed me to purchase the Fillmore Recreation Center and its adjoining land for the sum of 3.5 million dollars. I believe you'll find that's five hundred thousand dollars higher than Webster Development offered you. It's all outlined in the proposal."

Tom Riley flipped through the documents. "Does the proposal say what the foundation wants to do with the property, Mr. Whittaker?"

Whittaker looked at his own copy of the document and began pacing slowly in front of the council bench. "As you may know, the Universal Press Foundation publishes the *Universal Encyclopedia*, a resource dedicated to the excitement of learning. UPF proposes to rebuild the Fillmore Recreation Center—and I'm quoting now—as 'a place of adventure and discovery, filled with books and activities, fun and games, arts and crafts, and uplifting conversation.' But most of all, it will be a place where kids—of all ages—can just be kids." Whittaker stopped pacing and looked up. "I'd say that beats a video arcade, wouldn't you, Mr. Glossman?"

Say something! "W-why, this . . . this is preposterous! The Universal Press Foundation wants that old building when it could obviously build a brand-new one?"

Whittaker put his hands on the council bench and

leaned forward. "There are some people, Mr. Gloss-man, who like the old things, who don't want their town to be made of glass and chrome." He paused, then smiled and added, "Besides, what do you care, so long as the place gets sold? I mean, that *is* your objective, isn't it?"

CHAPTER THREE

The present . . .

Glossman looked down at his windowsill. A dead fly lay there on its back, legs in the air. *A stark reminder of how short life is,* he thought. At least it was for Jenny Whittaker. Glossman felt a sudden pang of sadness, and it surprised him. As he recalled, at the time of Jenny's death, he felt elated; his last obstacle to getting the

Fillmore Recreation Center was gone. But he couldn't forget the sight of Whittaker holding her there on the council-room floor.

A sudden stab of anger replaced his pang of sadness. The vote should have been just a formality. It was all supposed to be a formality that night! Only a miracle could have stopped him. And as it turned out, a miracle is just what happened.

Glossman glowered at the memory. Whittaker had trumped him. He could do nothing but sit there, turning red, with egg all over his face. Riley, of course, immediately called for a vote, and everyone agreed instantly, like the weak-minded bootlickers they were. And in the end, even he himself voted aye, making his humiliation complete. Then again, he had no choice; Whittaker had satisfied all of the council members' requirements, including Glossman's. Not voting aye would have made him look even more foolish.

The thing that really frosted him was finding out later that Whittaker actually *owned* Universal Press Foundation. Whittaker and Riley had played him like a fine violin. And because of it, he was stuck in Odyssey. His eyes narrowed. One day those two would have to be dealt with. They would have to pay for what they did and were still doing to him. And soon. Maybe that's what the call, if it ever came, was about.

It was getting dark outside. The street below was completely empty now; the shops were all closed up, and the streetlights were flickering to life. His belly emitted the loudest rumble yet, and the phone still didn't ring. And he couldn't get the image of Whittaker holding his dying wife out of his mind. Glossman crossed to his desk, sat down, opened the bottom drawer, and pulled out an old-fashioned pocket watch—the kind with a cover attached to a chain with a fob. He clicked it open. The watch didn't work, and the crystal was cracked, but that wasn't why he kept it. He kept it because of the small picture on the inside of the cover.

Lizzy.

She gave him the watch as a combination college-graduation-going-away present. He had graduated, but she went away, back home to England. He studied the picture—her golden-blonde hair, shining blue eyes, and radiant smile. They'd loved each other, but she wanted a simple life, and he wanted to rise in the business world. In the end, love wasn't enough, so she went to her simple life, and he wound up in Odyssey.

He sighed. If only he hadn't been so stubborn. Things could have been different. They could have had a life together. They could have been happy. They could have been like—the Whittakers.

Ruuuuuuummmble.

"That's it," he said aloud. "I've had enough!" He took one more look at Lizzy, clicked shut the cover, and put the watch in his waistcoat pocket, threading the fob through a buttonhole. He didn't care how good the money was. He wasn't going to continue being a puppet.

He stood, crossed to the coatrack, and retrieved his coat. "I'm not waiting around any longer," he muttered as he put it on. "I'm getting out of here for good. First I'm going to get some food, and then I'm going to quit the city council. Then I'm going to leave this wretched place, go to England, find Lizzy, and beg her to take me back. We'll get married and have children and live in the country so far away from everything and everybody that no one will ever be able to find us. Especially *him*!" He put his hand on the doorknob and turned it—

Riiiing!

Glossman jumped, startled. It was the call. It was *him.*

Riiiing!

He took his hand off the doorknob and looked at the phone.

Riiiing!

Maybe it wasn't *him*. Maybe it was someone else—a solicitor or—

Riiiing!

They say after four rings, if there's no answer, the caller usually hangs up—

Riiiing!

It was no use. Glossman walked slowly back to the desk and lifted the receiver.

"This is Glossman."

"Hello, Philip." The deep, dark voice fairly oozed out of the receiver. *His* voice.

Glossman swallowed. "H-hello, sir."

"Is everything all right? You sound tense."

"Everything is fine, sir. I'm just a little hungry."

"I'm so sorry to have kept you from your supper! Well, this won't take long."

"It's all right, sir. I figured it must be pretty important for you to, you know, call and everything." Glossman began to sweat.

"Oh, it is. Indeed it is. I know I've kept you in Odyssey for a long time—in part because of your blunder with the Fillmore Recreation Center, but for other reasons as well."

"O-other reasons, sir?"

"Yes. You've been very patient, Philip. And that patience is about to be rewarded. A great many things are headed your way. You're about to become *useful* again."

Glossman brightened, and he smiled. "Really, sir? Thank you! W-what kinds of things, if I may ask?"

"First, Webster Development is looking for another property in Odyssey. They'll require your assistance."

"Of course. May I ask what kind of property they'll be needing?"

"Something functional. And amusing. With a good line of sight to Whittaker's place."

"Understood."

"Next, Philip, I need you to find and make contact with a young man who lives in your town. He has recently come to my attention, and he possesses certain skills that will also be quite useful in the coming days."

"What kinds of skills?"

"Computer programming, good looks, and—how shall I put it?—a certain charm. And most important, an almost complete lack of moral character."

"As you said, sir, quite useful. What is this young man's name?"

"Maxwell. Richard Maxwell."

Glossman wrote down the name. "Well, that shouldn't be too hard to remember. Once I make contact, what would you like me to do with him?"

"Put him to work, of course."

"Yes, sir. Um, doing what?"

The deep voice chuckled smoothly. "I have kept you out of things for a while, haven't I? Disrupting, Philip. You are to put Maxwell to work disrupting things. Especially things having to do with Riley and Whittaker."

"Right! Of course!" He scribbled *disrupt things* next to Maxwell's name. "Uh, sir, suppose this Maxwell doesn't want to work for us?"

"*Us*, Philip?"

"Uh, *y-you*. What if he doesn't want to disrupt things for you?"

"It's your job to persuade him, Philip. Make sure he *does* want to. Understood?"

"Yes, sir."

"Stay on Whittaker as well. Do some disrupting of your own—perhaps with those precocious employees of his."

"I'll get on it immediately."

"Excellent! Oh, and Philip?"

"Yes, sir?"

The voice changed. It was cold as death. "That's a very nice picture of Lizzy in your watch. It'd be a shame if something were to happen to it—or to her."

Glossman's mouth went dry. "H-how did you—"

"Don't ever again think of running away from me, Philip. I know where you live, and I know where Lizzy lives. I will *always* find you. Am I making myself clear?"

Glossman's hand began to shake. "Y-yes, sir. Quite clear."

The voice was instantly warm and oozing again. "Well, I won't keep you from your supper any longer. Eat hearty! I'll be in touch. Ta!"

The line went dead.

Glossman dropped the receiver; it clattered to the floor. His knees buckled, and he collapsed into his chair.

He was no longer hungry. In fact, his appetite had disappeared entirely.

CHAPTER FOUR

To say that Constance, known as Connie, Kendall was persistent would have been an extreme understatement, especially when it came to finding out things her friends didn't want her to know.

Not that she was nosy, exactly—just extremely curious, like most sixteen-year-olds. The place where she worked and the man who owned it only enhanced her curiosity. That place was Whit's End: a combination soda-shop-discovery-emporium-adventure-center bustling with kids and excitement. The owner behind all the delicious treats, activities, and excitement was one John Avery Whittaker, the Whit of the center's title—which is also what almost everyone in town called him.

Whit had turned the rec center into a strange and wonderful conglomeration of things: museum, penny arcade, bookstore, laboratory, workshop, and, of course, soda shop, with just a dash of carnival fun house thrown in for good measure. Some of its attractions included the state's largest handmade electric train set (with the cars made by the patrons themselves); Inventors' Corner, where kids made their ideas come to life; an audio production and broadcast studio, from which a program called KYDS Radio emanated; a little theater; a well-stocked library; and the Bible Room, where artifacts, museum pieces, displays, and Whit's incredible invention, the Imagination Station, helped the Bible and history come alive.

Things were never dull at Whit's End, and though Connie's main duties were behind the counter at the soda fountain, she was involved with almost every-thing that went on at the place. It was, she thought, the best job ever.

The job did have two minor frustrations, though. One was her fellow employee, Eugene Meltsner. He was a student at Campbell County Community College and was quite brilliant, she had to admit, but almost completely lacking in social skills. Not that he needed them to do what he did. Whit had hired Eugene to care for and maintain the emporium's multiple inventions and gizmos, and he was excellent at it, keeping them all in tip-top condition—a fact he was only too happy to remind her of whenever she made the occasional mistake.

Eugene enjoyed lording his gigantic intellect over others, especially her, even though he pretended to be above such mundane concerns. Despite this, she actually liked him, and between the two of them, they kept the place humming along nicely, freeing Whit to do all the things he did so well.

Not that Whit always told them what he was

doing—or at least he didn't tell her. And that was her other minor frustration. Her boss was so open about some things and so secretive about others. For instance, she knew Whit served in the navy in World War II. She knew he'd been a middle school teacher, owned a publishing company, and bought the building that became Whit's End to honor his wife, Jenny, who died while fighting to save it from being torn down. Connie also knew he had a double bachelor of arts degree in philosophy and literature from the University of Southern California, and that he had three grown children: Jerry, a soldier who died for his country; Jana, who was divorced and had two kids; and Jason, who was as secretive about what he did as his father sometimes was.

The past week was one of Whit's secretive times, and Connie's curiosity about what was going on with him nearly made her crawl out of her petite, five-foot-four-inch frame. The fact that Eugene didn't seem to care at all only made it worse. They were both behind the counter at Whit's End, or more precisely, Eugene was *under* it replacing a burned-out coil in the flat-top freezer while she handled the usual Friday-afternoon minirush.

"Oh, come on, Eugene, you have to at least admit it's a little unusual!" She tucked a loose strand of her brown hair back into its customary ponytail and pushed the sleeves of her green sweater back up on her arms. She rang up an ice-cream-cone purchase and handed the customer his change. "And fifty cents makes a dollar. Thanks."

Eugene's muffled voice floated up from behind the freezer. "Define *unusual*, Miss Kendall."

"*Unusual*, Eugene, as in *not usual*." Connie turned to see her customer waving his hand to get her attention. "Yes, sir?"

"Napkins, miss?"

"No, thanks, I have some," Connie replied, turning back toward the counter.

"I'm well aware of the definition of *unusual*, Miss Kendall," said Eugene. "I simply fail to see how it applies here."

"Um, miss?" The man waved frantically toward Connie again.

"Fail to see? Are you serious, Eugene?" The movement caught her eye. "Yes, sir?"

"I meant napkins for me," the man said.

"Oh! Sorry! Over there . . . end of the counter." She watched the customer walk out of earshot, and then she turned back to peer at Eugene through her almond-shaped, light-brown eyes. "This whole thing has me so distracted, I can't even wait on the customers right!"

Eugene slithered out from behind the freezer and stood. He was tall and thin and favored jeans, short-sleeved T-shirts, and vests. His thick, reddish-brown hair was so long in front, it almost covered his eyes—which was ironic, since he also wore large, round glasses. "Actually, I fail to see any variation from your normal level of customer-care proficiency," he said with a smirk.

"Oh, hardy, har, har," said Connie, wrinkling her nose at him.

Eugene rolled the freezer back in place and plugged

it in. It responded with a faint electric hum. "Good as new, to employ the colloquialism," he said, obviously pleased with himself. "But please do not restock it until the internal thermometer reaches ten degrees Celsius. That is the optimal temperature for ice cream to remain firm enough to scoop and yet still smooth."

She rolled her eyes. "Thank you, Professor Ice Cream. I already know that. I'm not a complete dolt. And don't say, 'How much of a dolt are you?'" She paused and took a deep breath. "Now, what about Whit?"

Eugene began packing up his tools. "What about him, Miss Kendall?"

"There's something going on with him! He's been staying here long after the shop has closed. And when I walked past late at night several times this week, all the lights were on!"

Eugene closed his toolbox and wiped his hands on a rag. "Obviously he's working on a new invention."

"In the *whole shop*? There's something else going on, Eugene. I'm dying to know what it is!"

"Then while you were on one of your late-night scouting jaunts, why didn't you simply go in and ask him?"

"I tried. He bolted all of the doors from the inside."

Eugene chuckled. "Then it's obviously none of our business, Miss Kendall. I'm sure if it's important, Mr. Whittaker will tell us when he decides to."

She sighed, exasperated. "Just the kind of attitude I'd expect from you. Aren't you even a little bit curious?"

"No." He stuffed the rag in his back pocket. "My curiosity is reserved for intellectual and academic mysteries, not personal ones."

"I should have figured."

"And I must say, Miss Kendall, your insatiable inquisitiveness seems rather incompatible with your newfound Christian faith. I recall hearing Mr. Riley quote a New Testament verse admonishing the faithful to make it their ambition to live a quiet life and mind their own business. Sound advice."

She started to answer but heard a familiar voice call her from across the room.

"Connie!"

She turned to see Whit walking toward them. His usual slight limp was a bit more pronounced today, and though he was smiling, his brow was furrowed. She instantly felt guilty for spying on him during the past week. So she acted as innocent as possible, which made her feel even more guilty. As a result, her voice was a high-pitched squeak. "Ah yes, Whit?"

"Could you manage the counter by yourself for a little while? I need to see Eugene in my office."

"Oh! Uh, sure, Whit."

Whit smiled again. "Thanks, Connie. Eugene?"

"Yes, sir, Mr. Whittaker! Coming right away."

Connie watched the two move across the room and climb the stairs until they were out of sight. It didn't seem fair, she thought as she wiped down the counter. Why did Eugene get to know what was going on, but not her? She felt another pang of guilt. Whit had been very good to her, and Eugene was right about curiosity and her newfound faith.

Newfound faith. So much had changed in the year and a half since she and her mom moved to Odyssey. Back then she didn't want to have anything to do with Christianity. All she really wanted was to get back to California. Now she felt God's presence in her life every day. How had that happened? She still marveled when she thought about it.

The little bell over the entrance to Whit's End tinkled as several kids opened the door and left. She smiled. She must have heard that bell a thousand times by now, but she'd never forget the first time she heard it.

CHAPTER FIVE

Eighteen months earlier . . .

Front Street. Where in the world was Front Street? For such a small town, Odyssey sure was easy to get lost in. Connie thought she was heading to the town center, but now she was in a park. There were kids everywhere—more than she had ever seen at any park back in Los Angeles. Not that she spent much time in parks; she preferred the beach.

Funny thing about these kids: they didn't seem to be *playing* in the park as much as walking *through* it. She passed a small grove of trees and saw why. Most of the kids were headed toward a large, colorfully painted, Victorian-style mansion in the center of a grassy field. The mansion had an inviting covered porch along its front, a turret tower on one side, and a huge, glass-paned arboretum greenhouse in the back. A large sign, also colorfully painted, next to the porch's front steps said "Whit's End." Obviously the owner liked puns. Maybe someone in there could tell her where Front Street was.

She climbed the steps leading up to the front door, peeked through the large window next to it, and instantly knew why so many kids were going inside: a big part of the bottom floor was an ice-cream shop and soda fountain. Kids and adults alike were enjoying a variety of sundaes, cones, and ice-cream sodas.

Connie tucked under her arm the want ads she

had been carrying, went back to the front door, and opened it.

Ding-ding-ding!

A very pleasant tinkling bell greeted her—along with three people staring at her expectantly: a young girl, a young boy, and between them, a stocky older man with longish silver-white hair; large, round, wire-rimmed glasses; and a bushy, white mustache. He wore a herringbone jacket over a red sweater-shirt, and brown corduroy pants.

She didn't know why they were all staring at her, but they seemed to be waiting for her to say something, so she did. "Uh, excuse me—"

The three of them leaned forward with wide-eyed anticipation and asked in unison, "Yes?"

This is getting weird, she thought but said aloud, "Could you tell me how to get to Front Street?"

"Aw." The two kids' excited expressions dropped, and their shoulders drooped. *Even weirder.*

"Did I say something wrong?"

The older gentleman stepped forward, smiling.

"Oh, no, no! In fact, you had perfect timing! I was just explaining how a lot of times a sense of adventure is hard to hold on to. But sometimes it's just a matter of how you look at things. You never really know where your next discovery will happen. Excitement could be waiting right on the other side of that door—and then you came in."

Weirder and weirder. "I'm sorry to be such a disappointment."

The man chuckled. "You're not. By the way, this is Bobby and Amanda, and my name's John Avery Whittaker. But most folks call me Whit."

"I'm Connie Kendall."

The two kids muttered a shy hello and then wandered off deeper into the building. The older man held out his hand. "Pleased to meet you, Connie!" They shook hands, and he added, "Now, what did you need again?"

"Front Street."

"Oh yes, that's right. Did you want North Front Street or South Front Street?"

She blinked, then took the newspaper want ads from under her arm and unfolded them. "Uh, I don't know. Wait—I've got it right here." She scanned the paper, found the ad, and read it aloud quickly. "Wanted. Part-time clerk. Apply at Fashion Center, 1539 *North* Front Street. Sorry. Guess I should've read it a little closer."

"No worries. You're looking for a job, eh?"

"Yeah, but just until I can get enough money for bus fare. I have to get back to Los Angeles."

"You have family out in LA?" asked Whit.

"Just my dad. But I don't see him much anymore since he and my mom—well, you get the idea." For some reason, she didn't want to say the word *divorced*. "Then Mom got this brilliant idea that we ought to get out of the big city." Why was she telling all of this to a complete stranger? "So . . . about North Front Street?"

Whit nodded. "Oh yes. Fashion Center. Have experience in the clothing business, do you?"

She took a deep breath. "Well, I've had a lot of

experience *buying* clothes. That ought to count for something."

He chuckled again. "Of course. So is this your first job?"

"No way. Last summer I was a waitress."

A gleam came into Whit's eyes, and his brows arched slightly. "Really? A waitress. Interesting."

She frowned. "Why is that interesting?"

"Oh, just because of some of the other want ads in the paper." He reached for it. "May I?" She handed it over, and he adjusted his glasses and scanned the page. "Like this one. Wanted: responsible student with pleasant personality to help run busy soda fountain."

This was getting frustrating. "Yeah, interesting. Listen, is it far from here?"

"What?"

"North Front Street!"

"Oh! No, no, not far."

This guy was clueless! "Great. So if you'll just point me in the right direction, I'll find it on my own."

Whit folded the newspaper and handed it back

to her. "Well, I suppose you could do that. Or if you wanted to, you could walk downtown to Miller's Department Store, pick up an apron and a Whit's End T-shirt, and then head back here."

Her expression must have conveyed her complete confusion, because Whit smiled and pointed at the paper. "That last ad I read—the one for the soda fountain—was mine."

Connie felt her jaw drop open and quickly closed it again with a brief headshake. "Wait. You're offering me a job? I haven't even filled out an application."

Whit shrugged. "I don't know what else I'd ask you. I already know where you're from, a little about your family, what kind of work you've done, what experience you've had. Is there something I missed?"

She suddenly realized *she* was the clueless one and chortled. "No, I guess not. And I get the feeling there isn't much of anything you *do* miss."

He smiled again. "I'll take that as a compliment."

A loud crash turned their heads. At the counter she saw a man about the same age as Whit—only balding, wearing spectacles, and dressed in overalls and a blue work shirt. He was holding an empty tray off of which three ice-cream sundaes had just slid and splattered onto the countertop. The man quickly set down the tray and attempted to fix the mess.

"Oops!" he drawled. "Sorry 'bout that! Those sundae dishes are slipperier than, well, somethin' really slippery! Here, let me scoop that back into your cup. You all don't mind mixin' your ice cream together, do you?"

Connie looked back at Whit, who smiled sheepishly. "That's Tom Riley. He's, uh, helping. So, do you think you could start right away?"

She stifled a smile. "Can I at least ask how much the job pays?"

Whit scratched his chin thoughtfully. "Pay? Well, let's see. Tell you what. Why don't I call Marla down at the Fashion Center and ask her how much she plans to pay her part-time clerk. Whatever sounds fair to her sounds fair to me. Does that work for you?"

From the counter Tom shouted, "It works for me! Take the job!"

Whit chuckled. "Well?"

She was still hesitant, unsure. What was she getting herself into? She really didn't know this guy. On the other hand, she wouldn't know Marla at the Fashion Center either. Whit seemed friendly and likable enough, and the building was cool and filled with kids, so she wasn't worried about her safety. But she had already told him more about herself in the few minutes since they'd met than she'd told most of her friends back in Los Angeles before she left. He seemed like one of those people who wanted to build relationships. She didn't want or need a relationship. Yet she did want and need a job. And she had a sure one here that was likely to pay as much as any other job she'd be able to find in this town. All she had to do was say yes.

She took a deep breath. "Well, I guess I could try it."

Whit grinned broadly. "Good!" He turned and addressed the soda shop. "Hey, everybody. Listen up!"

The bustling room quieted down. "Say hi to Connie Kendall. She'll be helping me out here in the ice-cream department."

The room erupted in a cheer, which was cut short by a blender squealing, churning, and then erupting the contents of a chocolate shake all over the counter, the floor, and Tom Riley. He blinked several times. "Whoooo-wee!" he exclaimed, with liquefied chocolate ice cream dripping off the end of his nose. "This blender's got a mind of its own!"

Whit sighed. "And not a moment too soon."

Connie burst out laughing, and Whit, Tom, and the whole room joined her.

CHAPTER SIX

The present . . .

That was the beginning, Connie thought, *the start of a
fantastic journey.* She had no inkling then just how
fantastic it would be. A shiver went down her spine
when she thought of how close she came to taking a job
at the Fashion Center, which had since closed down.

The soda fountain was really emptying out now—

just a couple of lingerers left. She flipped a towel over her shoulder, grabbed a plastic tub, and made her way around the counter to bus the tables. The room took on that weirdly wonderful stillness and golden hue created by the setting sun.

Connie wondered if it would be another late night for Whit, or whether his asking Eugene up to his office meant that whatever project he was working on was finally finished. She set the tub on a table and looked over at the stairs again. The way the sunlight hit them, they seemed to shimmer and glow. She frowned. What was taking them so long up there? What was the big secret? And why did Whit trust Eugene with it more than her? She had half a mind to tromp up there, burst into the office, and demand—

No. She turned back to her work. She wouldn't let herself think that way. She had to trust that Whit had good reasons for what he was doing. He always did, even if he didn't let her in on the reason at first—or ever. She had seen it happen dozens of times with the kids at Whit's End. Somehow, with Whit, things always seemed to turn out all right—and mostly because he planned it that way. It was weird. She didn't know how he did it.

She stopped wiping off a table midswipe. Or maybe she *did* know how he did it, a little bit, because of what happened last December—the best, most wonderful, awesome thing that ever could have happened to her, or to anyone, for that matter. Not that Whit caused it exactly, but he certainly played a big part in it—or, as he would say, he was *allowed* to play a big part in it. And that was it—that was how he did all of the amazing things he did with the kids, with the town, and with her, she realized. He allowed his talents, his abilities, his smarts, and his very *self* to be used for good.

It seemed weird to think that allowing yourself to be used was not only the correct course of action; it was also the very best course of action. Yet what she had just realized was that it all depended on who was doing the using. That was Whit's secret. That was why he could take an old, run-down building and turn it into one of the most popular places around. And why he always seemed to have just the right words or advice at just the right time. And why he was so loving and kind and forgiving.

She also realized it was what had made her tell Whit so much about herself on their first meeting. Up until she met him, she had never known a true Christian. Oh, she had met people who called themselves "believers," and she had even been to church with some of them on Sundays. Then she'd see them during the rest of the week behaving worse than nonbelievers did, and she dismissed their so-called belief as nothing more than posturing and posing.

But Whit not only believed it; he lived it all day, every day. And so did Tom Riley, who turned out to be not nearly as inept and bumbling as he first seemed—far from it, in fact. She had no way then of understanding what she now knew fully: that in them she was seeing two true knights of faith that God had used to slowly make her a knight of faith as well. Or, at least, a knight in waiting. What were they called? Squires? She chuckled and shook her head. Knights and squires—

even her vocabulary had changed since she'd come to town.

She stacked several dirty sundae dishes in the bin and wiped down the table. As she moved to the next one, a new thought struck her: Whit's faith also explained why he seemed to know what would happen when she finally went back to California six months ago. She smiled as she remembered how much she had wanted to go back—or thought she did. From the moment she set foot in Whit's End, her only thought—obsession, really—was to get back to Los Angeles. Get away from the kids, the noise, the town, and especially all of the Christianity stuff. She'd be back where she belonged: on the beach with her group, soaking up the sun during the day and partying at night. She couldn't wait to get on the bus!

But almost as soon as she did, weird things started happening. First, Whit had given her a Christmas present and told her not to open it until she left town. When she did, it was—surprise—a Bible. When the girl who sat next to her saw it, she obviously thought

Connie was a religious nut and actually got up and moved. Then Connie fell asleep and awoke to find an elderly lady, Mrs. Nelson, sitting next to her. She quickly discovered that Mrs. Nelson was a Christian.

She thought she'd finally get back in California mode when she was on the beach with her friends. But when she got there and hung out with them, all she could think of or talk about was Odyssey, Whit, and Tom—a fact her friend Marcy pointed out with more than a little sarcasm. Then Connie learned that Pamela, the hardest-partying friend in her California group, had become a Christian. Pamela herself confirmed it when she visited Connie at her dad's place. Connie couldn't believe it. Not Pamela!

The topper came that night at a bonfire party on the beach that Pamela invited her to. Sitting by the fire, as pleasant as you please, was Mrs. Nelson, the Christian lady from the bus. Connie remembered thinking it had to be a conspiracy—Whit was tag-teaming all of his Christian forces to stalk her.

But as Pamela and Mrs. Nelson pointed out, it

wasn't Whit. It was a much greater force—a force Connie had been fighting against fiercely, until she could fight no longer. So she came back—to Odyssey, to Whit's End, to the kids and the noise and the Christianity stuff.

And back to her boss.

✜

Last December . . .

"Hi, Whit."

He was seated at his desk, but he instantly jumped up, mouth open in surprise, eyes wide. "Connie!" He rounded the desk and gave her a huge hug. "But . . . what are you doing here? You aren't supposed to be back for another two weeks!"

"I needed to come back early. Can we talk? Privately?"

He nodded. "Let's go to the Bible Room. It's been empty since Eugene set up the Spanish Inquisition display. The kids have been too scared to go in."

Eugene shrugged. "I thought some church history would be appropriate."

She didn't know what any of that meant, and at that moment, she didn't care. Her mind was still swimming. She thanked Eugene, who went back downstairs (how could he see through all that hair?), and then she followed Whit to the Bible Room. Appropriate.

Whit turned to her, seeming apprehensive. "Connie, I have to be honest. My heart is racing like a dozen horses. What did you want to talk to me about?"

She took a deep breath and looked right into his eyes, those piercing eyes. "I-I've been doing a lot of thinking, Whit. About Odyssey, Whit's End, going to California—lots of things." She wanted to pace, but she forced herself not to. She kept looking at Whit. "I think you know I've been feeling very confused over the past few months, and, well, I thought by going to California, everything would become clear for me. I could be myself, and I wouldn't be confused anymore. And you know what? That's exactly what happened.

I've got it all figured out, and now I know what I want to do."

Whit wet his lips nervously and gave a tentative nod. "Okay. What would you like to do?"

Could she say it? She didn't want to. But she knew she had to. "I want . . . I want to pray with you."

She sucked in a quick breath, astonished. Now that she'd finally said it, she wondered why it had taken her so long and was so hard to say. Pray! Of course she wanted to pray. It was the most natural thing in the world.

Whit was thunderstruck. "Pray?"

She nodded. "Yes. I'm not sure of all the right words. You know: forgive me for my sins, and, well . . . Whit, I want to ask Jesus Christ to come live in my heart."

He lowered his head for a moment, and when he looked up again, she got her biggest surprise of the past year's incredible journey—and yet when she thought about it, it wasn't a surprise at all. Her boss, her mentor, her teacher, her friend John Avery Whittaker was crying.

"Oh, Connie. Connie, you don't know how I've prayed to hear you say those words."

She smiled and squeezed his hand. "Yes, I do. I think your prayers made it all the way to California."

He chuckled through his tears, and she loved him for it.

"This may sound kind of hokey, Whit, but can we get on our knees?"

"That doesn't sound hokey at all."

They sank to their knees. She was excited, almost giddy, but not a silly kind of giddy. As odd as it seemed, she realized her giddiness came out of a sense of overwhelming peace. Her mind was still swimming, but instead of things being muddled and confused, everything was so clear, as though she had finally, at long last, come into herself—her real self. She didn't understand it, but she also knew she didn't have to. That it was happening was enough.

In front of her, Whit, still weeping with joy, whispered, "Thank You, Father God, thank You, thank You."

She took his hands in hers. "Are you ready?"

"If you are, dear one."

They bowed their heads. She took a breath.

"Dear Jesus . . ."

CHAPTER SEVEN

The present . . .

And just like that, she was changed forever.

Connie Kendall became a new creation.

It was the sweetest, best memory of her life, and yet her life since then had just gotten better and better. Yes, she had setbacks—mainly in the form of arguments with Eugene—but she had also learned so much about what it means to be a Christian. She had even led Bible studies with the kids. She didn't mind being around them anymore, either. In fact, a few of them—Donna Barclay, Lucy Cunningham-Schultz, and Robyn Jacobs—had actually become her good friends. She found new friends her own age at school and church as well.

Connie got to witness, and even participate in, most of the incredible things Whit was doing at Whit's End (okay, with Eugene's help), including the creation of his greatest invention yet: the Imagination Station, a strange and amazing device that let people experience events from the Bible and history firsthand. Wild!

It was safe to say, without a doubt, that this was the happiest she had ever been.

Even if she wasn't privy to everything Whit was doing.

And Eugene *was*.

The front door opened and the doorbell tinkled. Connie couldn't see the entryway from where she was standing. Who would be coming in now? It was late, the sunlight had completely gone, the soda fountain was empty, and she was getting ready to shut it down for the night. The door closed, and the visitor rounded the corner and came into view.

It was councilman Philip Glossman.

Connie was so taken aback, she dropped a soiled sundae dish into the tub. It clattered against the others but didn't break.

At the sound the councilman spotted her, raised a hand in greeting, and smiled. "Hello!"

Whit had told her all about Philip Glossman. He was the guy who tried to have the building in which they were standing torn down to put up a strip mall. The guy whom Whit's wife, Jenny, had battled until she literally collapsed on the city-council chamber floor and later died. Connie couldn't remember ever seeing him come in before. She felt an immediate dislike for him, but she tried to keep her expression passive and her voice as polite as possible. "Mr. Councilman."

Glossman looked pleasantly surprised and took a few steps toward her. "I'm flattered! I wouldn't expect very many people your age to know who I am, uh, Connie."

He knew her name? How did he know her name? "Yes, that's right. Now, *I'm* flattered."

His smile widened. "Don't be." He pointed to her shirt. "It's on your name tag."

Of course it was—she was such an idiot. She willed herself not to look down at her own name and make herself look like an even bigger idiot. Her dislike of him deepened with each passing moment, but she half chortled. "Ha! Right. Well, I was just about to shut down the soda fountain for the night, but I can still get you something if you like."

He shook his head. "No, no, nothing, thank you. I actually came by to see if your boss is all right."

She blinked. "All right?"

"Yes, you know . . . in good health."

Her brow furrowed. "Yeah, of course he is. Why wouldn't he be?"

Glossman's gaze wandered lazily around the room. "Oh, I just haven't seen him at very many city-council meetings lately." His gaze returned to her. "He's usually a regular." His expression changed to one of concern. "Of course, given his history in the council chamber, I'm rather surprised he *ever* goes to the meetings. You *do* know what happened there, don't you? With his wife?"

She stared daggers at him, though her expression didn't change. "Yes, I know." She almost added, ". . . what *you* did to her," but she stopped herself.

He looked down and shook his head sadly. "Tragic."

Her dislike was morphing into loathing. He was so fake. Did he really think she was buying this act?

He looked back at her. "So Whittaker's all right, then?"

"He's fine. He's just been busy lately." Why did she tell him that?

His eyebrows rose. "Oh? With what?"

She forced a smile and tried to keep her voice light. "Oh, you know Whit . . . uh, Mr. Whittaker. He's always working on some project or another."

Glossman smirked. "Yes. Always working well into the night."

Why did he say that? Had he been spying on Whit? She felt a flash of anger and then a pang of guilt. If he *had* been spying, she couldn't exactly fault him for doing something she had also been doing.

He leaned in conspiratorially. "I guess what he's working on is top secret, eh?" He was trying to charm her, but he was too unctuous.

She took a breath. "Mr. Councilman . . ."

He pulled back and chuckled. "I'm just teasing. Is he here now? Could I see him?"

"No, he's in a meeting." *Be quiet, Connie. Stop telling him things!*

His brows rose again, and he retrieved a pocket watch from his waistcoat and checked it pretentiously. "Really? This late? Must be with someone important."

Before she could stop herself, she scoffed. "No, he's just with Eugene."

He replaced the watch. "Eugene? Oh yes, the other employee."

How did he know *that*?

Then he added, "The brainy one."

She stiffened. What was *she*—chopped liver? She'd had enough of this pompous windbag. She opened her mouth to tell him to leave, when he surprised her.

"I'm sorry; that didn't come out right. Not that *you* aren't brainy as well. I'm sure you're Eugene's equal in every way."

She seethed. Got *that* right!

Glossman smiled. "Well, I won't keep you. Please tell Whittaker I stopped by. Give him my best and tell him I hope to see him at the next city-council meeting." He turned and headed toward the front door, where he stopped and turned back. "And Connie, sincerely, Whittaker is a fair and decent man, one of the most decent I've ever known. He'll do right by you, I'm sure. I really wouldn't read too much into him meeting with Eugene without you."

She smiled as brightly as she could. "Don't worry, Mr. Councilman. I won't."

He gave her a slight nod, turned again, and was

out the door. She watched him from the front window as he cantered down the steps and strolled off into the dusk.

It was all she could do to keep from throwing a sundae dish after him.

She whipped around and looked up the stairs. She couldn't believe it. She wouldn't believe it. But Eugene was up there, and she was down here.

She sank into a chair, ashamed, hating herself for what she was thinking. Her eyes welled with tears, and she lowered her head. "Dear God," she whispered, "please help me."

CHAPTER EIGHT

A half hour earlier . . .

Whit and Eugene made their way to Whit's office, a cozy, comfortable room, tastefully decorated with wood-paneled wainscoting and pictures of his family and friends on the one wall not taken up by bookshelves and a fireplace. A large oak desk sat in front of an impressive bay window with a lovely view of

McAlister Park and the town of Odyssey beyond it. Whit entered and moved to a large bookcase near the office door. "Come in, Eugene."

"Yes, sir."

"You'd better close the door."

"Oh. Yes. Of course." Eugene pushed the door closed and turned back to his boss, who seemed to be examining him carefully. Eugene had the sensation of being under a microscope. He cleared his throat. "Um . . . is everything all right, Mr. Whittaker?"

Mr. Whittaker looked apprehensive, as though he was about to do something he didn't want to do but also knew he needed to do. He inhaled deeply and said, "Eugene, I want you to take a good look at this bookcase."

Eugene blinked. "The . . . bookcase?"

"Yes."

Eugene wasn't quite sure what to do or say. He gave the bookcase a quick once-over. "It's . . . it's a very nice bookcase, Mr. Whittaker."

Mr. Whittaker chuckled. "Thank you, but I'm not

looking for compliments, Eugene. I want you to make note of a particular book—right here—*The Last Battle* by C. S. Lewis. See it?"

"Yes, sir. *The Last Battle*."

Mr. Whittaker took the book from its place on the shelf and opened it. "This book has a secret: there's a key on the inside front cover."

"A key."

"Yes." Mr. Whittaker held it up. It was an old-fashioned caboose key, an oval on one end connected by a thin rod to a small hatchet shape on the other end, with symmetrical cuts in the blade. "See? And as soon as I put it in this lock—right here next to the bookcase—you'll see what the key is for and why I hide it." He started to insert the key in the lock and then stopped. "Tell you what. It'll be better if you do it." He handed Eugene the key.

"Oh! Right." Eugene stepped up to the lock and inserted the key in the hole. It fit perfectly. "You know, Mr. Whittaker, I've often wondered why you had a keyhole next to this bookcase."

Mr. Whittaker smiled. "Turn the key, and you'll find out."

Eugene did as he was told. There was a metallic click, and the whole bookcase moaned and moved aside, as though on a hinge. The shelves concealed a whole other room. Eugene smiled. "Ah! There's a hidden room behind the bookcase. Very clever! It brings to mind an old-fashioned mystery novel—not that I've ever read one myself."

Mr. Whittaker looked into the room. "I had it built when I moved into the building. Come in. I have some things to show you."

A low electronic hum came from the room and increased in volume as they entered. The room was about the size of a large walk-in closet, and electronic equipment lined an entire wall of it from floor to ceiling. The equipment beeped softly. Small screens glowed in various places, and a large screen stood in the center. Tiny lights on it blinked randomly. Eugene felt his heart flutter. "Excellent, Mr. Whittaker! State-of-the-art, if I may say."

Mr. Whittaker nodded. "That's one reason why the room is hidden." He turned to the largest screen. "Hello, Mabel."

The screen lit up, and as the lights blinked and flashed, a mechanical yet feminine voice responded, "Hello, John Avery Whittaker."

Eugene's jaw dropped. "It talks no less!"

Mr. Whittaker nodded again. "I've installed components for voice activation and artificial intelligence."

Eugene felt as though hearts were floating from his eyes to the machine. "I'm *extremely* impressed! Is this what you've been working on for the past few weeks?"

"Partly. Have a seat, Eugene. There's more you need to know."

Eugene pulled up a chair and sat as Mr. Whittaker turned back to the screen.

"Mabel, load program menu please."

The screen blinked, lights flashed, and words appeared on the screen. "Program menu loaded." Mr. Whittaker turned to Eugene. "Do you remember when you first started working here, how you computerized all of the trains and displays in the Bible Room?"

Eugene lowered his gaze slightly. "Yes, sir. You weren't particularly pleased and had me dismantle them."

Mr. Whittaker put a hand on his shoulder. "And I'm sure you recall why. Everything was so computerized, the kids couldn't enjoy themselves. But that didn't mean your idea was a bad one. So I've computerized everything again—not to take it away from the kids, but so we can see which displays they're using and which ones they aren't."

Eugene perked up. "I see. You can determine which ones they like and which ones they don't."

"Exactly. We'll also be able to turn everything on and off from this computer if absolutely necessary."

Eugene quickly perused the program menu. "Yes—the train set, the Bible Room mirror, Noah's ark, headsets, the Imagination Station, the Environment Enhancer."

Mr. Whittaker smiled. "Everything's there."

"Very efficient." Then Eugene noticed it. "What's this program, Mr. Whittaker? Applesauce."

Mr. Whittaker took a deep breath, and his smiled faded. "I can't talk about that one, Eugene," he said seriously. "And you shouldn't ever touch it or try to use it."

Eugene sat back in his chair and frowned. "Really? Why not, if I may ask?"

"You may ask, but I can't tell you."

Eugene's eyebrows rose. "A top-secret program of some sort?"

Mr. Whittaker scowled. "Something like that. Just stay away from it. You can use all the others, but not that one. Understand?"

Eugene had never seen Mr. Whittaker this serious before. He gulped and nodded. "Yes, sir. Understood."

Mr. Whittaker's demeanor softened a bit. "I'm showing all of this to you as a matter of trust, Eugene. I don't want anyone else to know this room exists. I thought you should know about it just in case anything should happen to me. You're the only one who would know how to use this room properly."

Eugene felt pride swell in his chest. "I'm honored, Mr. Whittaker. Very honored." He turned to the screen. "Mabel, it is a pleasure to meet you."

The machine's lights blinked and flashed. "Likewise, I'm sure."

Eugene's face lit up like the machine. "Oh, how clever!"

Mr. Whittaker laughed.

✦

They stayed in the computer room for about a half hour, and Mr. Whittaker showed Eugene a few more programs and functions Mabel could perform. Finally Mr. Whittaker decided to call it a night. They left the room, and Mr. Whittaker closed the bookcase and locked it, placing the key in *The Last Battle* and the book in its proper spot on the shelf. Mr. Whittaker told Eugene he had more work to do in the office, and Eugene took that as his cue to leave his boss alone.

Eugene closed the office door behind him, marveling at what he had just seen and experienced. He felt immense gratitude toward Mr. Whittaker for entrusting him with such an important and incredible secret and wished he were better at expressing such mundane emotions.

He made his way down the hallway toward the Train and Bible Rooms to shut them down for the evening, when he remembered that he didn't need to do that anymore. Mabel would do it for him. He was quite gratified that Mr. Whittaker saw the wisdom of placing all of the attractions and devices at Whit's End under the control of a central computer system. That was the first idea Eugene had when he came to work there, and he knew it was a good one. He regretted that his boss took so long to process the idea, but he knew

Mr. Whittaker wasn't the kind of man who would let a good idea go to waste.

The front-door bell downstairs tinkled, and his thoughts drifted back to the days when he was first hired. That bell also fell under his watchful eye—and ear.

CHAPTER NINE

Six months earlier . . .

Eugene opened the front door of Whit's End, and the tinkling of a bell met his ears. *Pleasant enough,* he thought, *but hardly efficient.* He quickly surveyed the room—a rather quaint, old-fashioned ice-cream shop filled with youngsters, with a counter at the far end, where two older gentlemen stood, one balding with spectacles and wearing overalls, and the other wearing a herringbone jacket over a red sweater-shirt, with a mane of silver-white hair, round glasses, and a bushy, white mustache.

Eugene crossed the room and approached the men, putting on his cheeriest attitude. "Good day, gentlemen!"

"Hi," said Mr. Mustache.

"Hello," said Mr. Overalls.

"There's a more efficient way to let you know a customer has come in than that small bell above the door."

Mr. Overall's eyebrows rose, and Mr. Mustache looked bemused. "Probably. Are you a salesman?"

"No, sir. My name is Eugene Meltsner, and I'm a science student and recognized genius at the Campbell County Community College. Whom do I have the pleasure of addressing?"

Mr. Mustache said, "I'm John Whittaker, and this is Tom Riley."

"Howdy," Mr. Riley said cheerfully.

Eugene's brain whirred. "Howdy. An abbreviated form of the phrase 'How do you do?' or in the older English, 'How do you fare?' In answer, I fare well, thank you."

Mr. Riley's eyes narrowed. He leaned over to Mr. Whittaker and muttered, "What'd he say?"

Mr. Whittaker muttered back, "I think he said he's fine."

"Did I ask?"

Mr. Whittaker chuckled. "I guess you did." In a louder voice he asked, "What can I do for you, Mr. Meltsdown?"

Eugene shook his head slightly. "Melts*ner*. Richard Pierce, my counseling professor at the college, suggested I speak to you. So I am."

"I see. Speak to me about what?"

The man seemed slow on the uptake. "Studying under you. Professor Pierce said that you are somewhat remarkable as an inventor and scholar, and that I would find your approach to life very—shall we say—different, if not altogether fascinating, and certainly beneficial to my pursuant education."

Mr. Riley again leaned toward Mr. Whittaker and muttered, "What'd he say?"

"I think he wants to work for me."

Eugene interjected, "*If* that's possible. Professor Pierce said I could receive class credits."

Mr. Whittaker exchanged glances with Mr. Riley and said, "Your timing couldn't be better, Hubert."

"Eugene."

"I happen to have an opening for part-time help. It's temporary, maybe through the holidays only, but—"

Eugene placed his hand over his heart and bowed slightly. "I would be proud and honored to offer my meager ministrations as your most obsequious journeyman for whatever course of time you deem necessary."

Mr. Riley looked utterly baffled. "Eugene, I can't understand a word you're saying. Are you one of those foreign-exchange students?"

Mr. Whittaker laughed. "Welcome to Whit's End, Eugene."

Eugene's mind whirred again. "Whit's End. Is that a pun?"

"Sort of."

"I hate puns."

"Oh."

✦

For the next hour or so, Mr. Whittaker let Eugene wander about the place on his own, soaking in the rooms and attractions. It was intriguing, to say the least—just the kind of place that could use his superior skills.

He made his way back to the soda counter. Mr. Riley was nowhere in sight.

Mr. Whittaker was finishing a telephone conversation. "Yes, Connie, I'll be at the bus station at 6:30 a.m. sharp. You don't think I'd let you slip out of town without saying good-bye, do you? Well, I'll be there anyway. See you in the morning. 'Night." He hung up the phone, sighed, and said softly, "Lord, help me relax about this. You love Connie even more than I do."

Eugene was taken aback. Was the man actually *praying*—a man of science and technology? "Uh, Mr. Whittaker?"

"Oh! Hello, Eugene. Please, call me Whit."

"I think nicknames are terribly disrespectful, Mr. Whittaker."

"Oh. Did you get a good look around the place?"

"I certainly did! It's a fascinating building you've assembled here. The Victorian architecture is a poor disguise for the marvels inside."

Mr. Whittaker smiled. "Does that mean you like it?"

"*Like* isn't a word I like to use. Let's just say I find this shop of yours to be a curiosity worth studying."

"Uh, thank you. I think."

"The train set is unlike anything I've ever seen. But do you realize that with a very simple computer program, you could operate those trains with far more efficiency and less wear?"

Mr. Whittaker nodded. "I considered that once, but with a computer program, the children wouldn't be able to run them."

"Precisely! I'll put the program together for you. It will take no time at all. Professor Pierce would be grateful for me to have the experience. *I'd* be grateful."

"Uh, grateful . . . of course."

"In fact, I've thought up *all kinds* of new ideas for your shop, to make it far more convenient and efficient for you *and* your customers, from ice-cream serving to the displays upstairs. After all, that's what inventing is about, isn't it, Mr. Whittaker?"

"In a way."

"I'll get started tonight, while the shop is closed. You'll be amazed when you come back in the morning!"

He hurried off toward the stairs. As he did, he thought he heard Mr. Whittaker mutter, "That's what I'm afraid of."

❖

Eugene worked like a whirlwind for the next week, and the results were remarkable, if he said so himself. The whole place had been automated, from the train set and the Bible Room to the pizza oven and milkshake machine. No human touch was necessary; computers ruled the roost. For Eugene, it was truly paradise.

Mr. Whittaker, however, had other ideas. At the end of the week, he approached Eugene in the Inventors' Corner.

"Eugene."

"Ah! Hello, Mr. Whittaker. I've been going over these plans, and I *think* I've determined a way to—"

"Eugene," Whit cut in, "we need to talk."

Eugene blinked. "We do?"

"Yes. It's about the *work* you've been doing."

Eugene knew what this was about—praise. He had faced this before and was uncomfortable dealing with such inanities. "Now, Mr. Whittaker, let's not resort to something so sentimental as gratitude. We're both men of science, and we use our talents to better the human race."

To his surprise, Mr. Whittaker's expression turned hard, his gaze piercing. "Time out. Everybody off the field."

"I-I beg your pardon?"

"Eugene, I *do* appreciate your efforts around the shop, but you're missing something *very important* in what you're doing."

"I hate to contradict you, Mr. Whittaker, but I am known for thoroughness. What could I have possibly missed?"

"Your *heart*."

Eugene blinked again, baffled. "I beg to differ. I couldn't function at all if my heart weren't—"

Mr. Whittaker shook his head. "Not your physical heart, Eugene. Your *emotional* heart. See, you've done a great job of automating everything around here. But Whit's End isn't about automation, machines, or inventions. It's about *people*. The kids come here for the fun—to learn, to build, but more important, to have human contact, a human touch. You can make it more efficient with your inventions, but can you make it warmer, friendlier, more *loving*?"

Eugene was completely taken aback. This had never happened to him before. "Does this mean you're firing me?"

Mr. Whittaker smiled and patted his shoulder. "No. It means that I want you to undo everything you've done. Then we'll see what we need to do *together*. Okay?"

He wasn't being fired—relief! "Certainly, Mr. Whittaker. I understand."

At that moment, a loud, obnoxious buzz from downstairs made them both jump. Mr. Whittaker pointed. "And the *first thing* you can do is put that nice little bell back above the front door!"

Eugene smiled sheepishly. "Yes, sir. Right away."

CHAPTER TEN

The present . . .

"**C**an you make it warmer, friendlier, more loving?"

Eugene stood in the middle of the Bible Room with Mr. Whittaker's words echoing in his mind. Warmer, friendlier, and loving were what this room was all about, he knew, but they weren't concepts with which he was comfortable, mainly because he didn't understand them. He had learned to tolerate them better during his tenure at Whit's End—mostly because of his work in this room—but he still preferred computers, science, and the accumulation of knowledge. These he understood well and was frequently astounded when others not only didn't understand them but also purposefully chose emotion instead.

People like Miss Kendall, for instance. He knew her to have a decent mind—nothing nearly as advanced as his, of course, but decent nonetheless. And yet, rather than develop her mind to its fullest potential, she so frequently opted to wallow in a vat of emotional soup. Her persistent curiosity regarding what Mr. Whittaker had been up to the past several weeks was a perfect example. Rather than imitate his cool, intellectual detachment, she preferred to obsess. Such irrationality led to the only place it could: her ultimate disappointment.

Not that her situation was completely devoid of emotion for him—namely, humor. He smiled, certain she was downstairs stewing at the reality that yet again he knew something she didn't, and despite himself, he took an admitted pleasure in that.

Then again, he didn't know *everything*, did he? His smile faded.

Applesauce.

The image of Mr. Whittaker's serious demeanor concerning the program popped into his mind and caused him no small amount of concern. It was one thing to have a computer control everything at Whit's End, but quite another thing for that computer to contain a program so top secret it couldn't even be discussed.

Why would Mr. Whittaker even put such a program on Mabel in the first place? There was obviously much more to his boss than he knew.

Eugene's brow furrowed. Curiosity suddenly welled up within him and nearly overwhelmed him. What could be on that program? He had to know! The next time Mr. Whittaker was away, he'd go up to the office, get the key, open the bookcase, and . . .

"What am I doing?" he said aloud. He examined

himself and was surprised to see his hands curled into fists, hear his breath whistle through gritted teeth, and feel his heart pound in his chest. He willed himself to calm down. When he regained composure, he had a startling thought: perhaps he wasn't that different from Miss Kendall after all.

He shuddered, shook his head, took a deep breath, did his best to wipe clean the memory of the past few moments, turned out the lights, and left the room.

CHAPTER ELEVEN

Richard Maxwell hated Fridays. And Saturdays.

More specifically, he hated Fridays when there was a holiday at Odyssey Middle School. Saturdays he just hated generally.

He worked part time at Odyssey Retirement Home. It was a quiet place most days, the exceptions being Saturday, when visitors came, and Friday school holidays, when even *more* visitors came. Like today, for instance. The schedule at the front desk revealed that a church youth group was coming to sit with the home's denizens, which meant he would have to be on his best behavior. He preferred the rest of the week—except for Saturday—and no holidays. He could get more work done that way.

He crossed the lobby, heading for the janitor's closet and his cleanup cart. He stopped at the door, ran his hand through his thick brown hair, and checked his reflection in the door's window. He was good looking, no doubt about that—perfect nose, perfect teeth, and soft brown eyes to match his hair. *I'm so pretty, I should kiss myself,* he thought, then laughed aloud at his own joke and opened the door. Too bad he had to wear that silly uniform, but it helped him blend in and get his work done without drawing any attention to himself.

He loaded up the cart with cleaning supplies, dust cloths, and trash bags, then chuckled. Work. If the management knew what kind of "work" he was *really* doing at the home, they wouldn't let him anywhere near the place.

The setup was so sweet. The old geezers just left their stuff lying around—easy pickings. Most of them didn't even notice their stuff was missing. If they did notice, all he had to do was make them think they had forgotten where they put their things, then get them to obsess about something else. Like that cranky biddy Mrs. Hooper, with her plants and her whining about how her daughter never visited her, and all the while, she left completely unguarded her *real* valuables—jewelry, knickknacks, and cash.

Still, he took only a little at a time and always things that could be easily "misplaced." He pocketed the cash and fenced the jewelry and knickknacks with Myron. Or what was he calling himself now? Jellyfish? It worked like a charm; he was making cash, and no one suspected a thing.

Richard heard a commotion in the lobby and poked his head out of the janitorial closet. The church youth group had arrived. An older guy with a bushy mustache and round glasses handed out visiting assignments to the kids. *Bunch of do-gooders,* he thought. He was about to retreat into the closet when he recognized one of them—a cute, young, freckled brunette. "Donna Barclay," he muttered. "She used to hang around with my sister."

Richard watched as Donna got a room number from the old guy, then turned away, looking nervous. She crossed the lobby toward his door. He was just about to open it and say something to her when another cute, young, glasses-wearing brunette about Donna's age rushed up to her. He quickly closed the door so they wouldn't see him but left it open a crack so he could still see and hear them.

"Donna!"

"Oh, hey, Lucy. Who did you get?"

Lucy held out her paper. "Mr. Morton in room 307. I've visited him before."

"You have? Is he nice?"

Lucy nodded. "Yeah, he's wonderful. He's ninety-seven years old and has all kinds of stories to tell."

Donna took a deep breath. "I've never done this

before. I'm kind of nervous. I hope I got someone who isn't too—you know—*old.*"

Lucy grinned. "Who did you get?"

Donna looked at her paper. "Umm. Room 754. Mary Hooper."

Lucy's grin faded. "Oh."

Donna looked up, brow furrowed. "What do you mean 'oh'? Have you visited her before?"

"Well . . . once."

"And?"

Lucy's face turned red. "And . . . I probably shouldn't say anything."

Donna grabbed Lucy's arm. "If you probably shouldn't say anything, then you probably should say something. What do you know about Mary Hooper? You're making me nervous!"

Lucy patted Donna's hand. "Don't be nervous. She was just a little difficult. Please don't make me say anything else. I'm sure deep down inside she's a very nice lady." She paused. "*Deep* down inside—*really* deep."

Donna paled. "Uh-oh."

"Maybe it was just me. She might like you." Lucy moved off, calling back as she went. "And whatever you do, don't touch her flowers and plants!"

Donna sighed deeply and stared at the paper again. Richard waited until he was sure Lucy had gone and then opened the door to the janitor's closet. "Hey, Donna."

"Huh?" She jumped, startled, then she recognized him. A look of extreme annoyance crossed her face. "Richard. What are you doing here?"

"I work here part time. I'm what you'd call an orderly." He pulled out his cart and closed the closet door.

Donna eyed the cart. "You look more like a janitor."

He shrugged. "One person's janitor is another person's orderly. You visiting with the church group?"

"Obviously."

"What room are you looking for?"

"Seven fifty-four."

"It's around this way. Not far. Come on, I'll walk you." He started pushing his cart.

Donna stayed put. "You don't have to," she said coldly.

"I'm going that way anyway." He stopped. "Look, I know you and my sister don't hang around anymore, but I'm just trying to help."

She sighed and slowly joined him. They headed down the hallway together in silence, walking past walls painted with colorful flowers, butterflies, and rainbows but rendered bland and joyless by the clinical, fluorescent lighting. He saw her glance at the paper again. "Did you say seven fifty-four?" he asked.

"Yes."

This ought to be fun, he thought. He whistled softly and shook his head. "Mary Hooper. What're you visiting her for?"

Her worried expression returned. "'Cause I got her name. Mr. Whittaker passed out residents' names when we got here."

"Is that it? You're visiting her just because you got her name?"

Now her face turned red. "Well, no. I mean, I want to talk to her and, you know, get to know her and be her friend and . . . stuff."

He smirked. "You're going to try to be friends with Mary Hooper? Forget it."

"Why?"

"'Cause she don't want friends."

She frowned. "I can try, can't I?"

He chuckled. "Sure you can try . . . but trying ain't *doing*." He rolled his cart to a stop in front of a wood-paneled door. "Here's her room." He grinned. "Do I get a kiss good night?"

She scowled. "Get lost, Richard."

He laughed and started pushing his cart again, calling back the way Lucy did. "By the way, Donna, don't touch her flowers and plants!" As he rounded a corner, he heard her take a deep breath and then knock on the door. "Give that about a half hour," he muttered, "and Mary Hooper will be ready to pluck again." He chuckled softly.

As it turned out, it took only twenty minutes.

Richard returned with his cart just in time to see Donna burst out of Mrs. Hooper's room and run down the hallway. He smiled and again felt the bag filled with "goodies" he had lifted from several other residents. He wheeled his cart toward room 754.

Easy pickings.

✤

Later that afternoon, a pair of gray eyes watched a good-looking young man with thick brown hair and wearing a janitor's uniform leave through the back door of Odyssey Retirement Home. The young man carried a small backpack, which he put in a carryall container attached to the back of a motor scooter. He climbed on the scooter, started it up, and took off.

The gray eyes belonged to Philip Glossman, who sat

in his car across the street from the retirement home's back door and observed Maxwell ride off. Glossman didn't follow; he didn't need to. He had already followed Maxwell three times and knew what he had in the backpack and where he was going with it. Glossman took a small notepad and pen from his pocket and recorded his observations.

"Stealing from old folks," he muttered, shaking his head. "It'll almost be a pleasure to hand this little twerp over to *him*."

CHAPTER TWELVE

Two weeks had passed since Glossman's surprise visit to Whit's End. Connie's memory of the unpleasant events of that afternoon and evening had faded some-what in the discovery emporium's usual daily hustle and bustle. There were no more late nights for Whit or private meetings between him and Eugene. Connie had told Whit about Glossman on the morning fol-lowing his visit, and he responded with mild interest.

This morning, Friday, Whit had taken a bunch of church kids, who were on a school holiday, to the Odyssey Retirement Home to visit the folks there. Whit and the kids had come back only a few minutes ago, and Whit left almost immediately to run some errands. It was late afternoon, and Connie and Eugene were slowly making the rounds, closing down unused rooms and attractions. She went into the Train Room to shut the train off and found Donna Barclay sitting alone watching the tiny cars go around the tracks. "Donna?"

"Hi, Connie."

"I thought you'd gone home. Everything okay?"

"Yeah. Just thinking."

"Didn't you go to the retirement home today?"

Donna nodded. "That's what I'm thinking about."

Connie also sat. "What happened?"

One of the little engines whistled. Donna blurted out, "The person I got was horrible!"

"Really?"

"Yeah! Her name is Mary Hooper, and she's a mean,

cruel, bitter old woman. And Lucy knew about her too but didn't tell me!"

Connie put a hand on Donna's shoulder. "How bad was she? Mrs. Hooper, I mean?"

Donna stood and started pacing. "She called me ignorant and a derelict and tried to show me her bruises from where she said they beat her with rubber hoses! I ran out of her room and just stayed on the bus until it was time to come back here."

Connie nodded sympathetically. "That's pretty bad, all right. And Lucy didn't say *anything*?"

Donna stopped in front of the train set and watched the tiny cars race around the tracks. "Well . . . I guess she did say that Mrs. Hooper was difficult. And Lucy and Richard both said not to touch her flowers and plants, so I suppose I should have taken that as a warning." She turned and faced Connie. "But I *didn't* touch them, and Mrs. Hooper was still horrible to me!"

"Richard? Richard who?"

Donna grimaced. "Richard Maxwell. He's an orderly slash janitor at the home."

"How do you know him?"

"Remember my friend Rachael? I hung around with her a lot a few months back."

Connie shook her head. "Vaguely."

Donna looked embarrassed. "She almost got me in trouble. Turns out she was pretty bad company. Anyway, Richard is her older brother. Well, half brother."

"Ah."

"That was another problem with today. It was weird seeing him there."

"Why?"

Donna shrugged. "I don't think he's great company either."

"He can't be all bad if he's working at the retirement home."

"Maybe. But knowing Richard, he's got something bad going." Donna sighed. "I guess seeing him just brought back some feelings I'd rather forget. And combined with Mrs. Hooper . . . it just wasn't a great day."

Connie rose and put her arm around Donna's

shoulders. "I'm sorry, Donna. But that's the nice thing about this place. You always have friends here."

Donna smiled. "I know." Another sigh. "I guess I'd better get home. Thanks, Connie."

"Anytime."

Donna picked up her bag and left the Train Room.

"And now I can turn off the train," Connie muttered. She looked around the set for the off switch but couldn't find it. It had been awhile since she'd done this; maybe she had forgotten where the switch was. Then she remembered. There wasn't a switch, just a plug. She rounded the table until she found the power cable, but it went under the big platform the train set sat on and right into the floor. "Hmm. No plug and no switch. Now what?"

She went to the door and yelled, "Eugeeeene—oh!" she jumped back, startled.

He was standing in the hallway. "No need to shout, Miss Kendall. I'm right here."

She slapped him on the arm. "You scared me! I wouldn't have shouted if I had known you were there."

He smirked. "That has not been my experience with you, but it is of no matter. How may I be of assistance?"

She let the slight pass. "I'm trying to turn off everything, but the train set won't."

"Won't what?"

"Fly to the moon," she said sarcastically. "Turn *off*, Eugene!"

"Ah. Did you try unplugging it?"

"Duh, yeah! But it doesn't unplug anymore. The cord goes through the floor." She pointed. "See? Whit changed it . . . among other things."

Eugene nodded knowingly. "Oh yes. That's true. Well, stay right here, and I'll see what I can do." He headed down the hallway.

"What do you mean *stay*? Where're you going?"

He kept moving away. "The office," he said over his shoulder.

She called after him. "The office? But the train set is in here!"

He stopped in front of Whit's office door and fished a set of keys from his pocket. "Yes, I know," he called back. "Wait right there." He found the right key, inserted it in the lock, opened the door, stepped inside, and closed it behind him.

Connie scowled, frustrated. "Wait right there," she muttered mockingly. Why wouldn't anyone tell her what was going on around here? Maybe Glossman, as loathsome as he was, was onto something. Maybe she and Eugene weren't equals after all.

She put her hands on her hips. *I'm getting tired of being left out of everything,* she thought. *Well, not this time!* "Eugene!" She stormed down the hallway toward the office. "Eugene! I want to know what you're doing! It's not fair!" She reached the office door, knocked, and without waiting, opened it and walked in. "I should be allowed to know what's . . . going . . . on." Her voice trailed off, and her mouth hung open.

The big bookshelf in Whit's office had moved aside, as though it was a door on a hinge. The shelves concealed a whole other room—a room filled with computer equipment. Eugene stood in front of the large screen and talked to it. "Mabel, please load program—"

"Eugene?"

He whipped around. "Miss Kendall! What are you doing in here?"

She was awestruck. "So *this* is what Whit has been working on? What *is* all this?"

Suddenly, to her further astonishment, the electronic equipment answered. "Please repeat command. I do not have program called 'Miss Kendall, what are you doing in here.'" The voice was female but metallic. Connie thought it sounded like a robot.

Eugene turned back to it. "Sorry, Mabel. Please load the program for the train set."

Beep. "Stand by."

He turned back to Connie. "Miss Kendall, you're not supposed to be in here. Mr. Whittaker made it very clear—"

"It's a big computer, isn't it? Does it operate the whole shop?"

Beep. "Train-set program loaded."

"And it talks, too!"

"Yes!" Eugene looked flustered. "Miss Kendall, I could get in big trouble for this."

She waved him off and moved farther into the room. "No you won't. I came in on my own. You can't help it if I saw all this." The blinking and beeping were mesmerizing. "This is *incredible*. I mean, I've seen laptops and even big computers before, but this looks like something out of a spaceship."

Eugene huffed and then turned to the computer. "Mabel, please turn off the train set."

Beep, blink, boop, whir. "The train set is off."

He turned back to Connie. "There. The train set is off. There is no reason for us to remain—"

"I want to see more! What else does it do?"

"Miss Kendall—"

She folded her arms adamantly. "I'm not leaving until you show me, so you may as well just save your breath."

He sighed. "Child."

She stuck out her tongue at him. "Sticks and stones. What else does it do?"

"Mabel, program menu on screen, please."

Beep. "Program menu on screen."

Connie giggled. "How does it do that? Talk, I mean."

"Artificial intelligence," Eugene said haughtily. "Something I'm sure you wouldn't know about."

"I know about it!" she sneered. "It's, uh, intelligence that's . . . that's—"

"Artificial?" He smirked.

"Exactly! Kind of like artificial Christmas trees. They're fake. They're made to seem like the real thing, but they aren't."

He emitted a soft, condescending hiss. "In its most simplistic definition, I suppose you're close enough."

If she could actually have seen his eyes behind all that hair, she was sure they were rolling. She didn't care; Mabel was too fascinating. The big screen in front of them displayed a long list, and she recognized almost everything on it. "Look at all the programs. It has everything in the shop, even the kitchen appliances!"

Eugene nodded curtly. "It's a master control. May we please go? If Mr. Whittaker comes back now—"

A new program caught her eye. "Hey, what's this one?" She pointed. Eugene leaned in.

It was a program called Applesauce.

Eugene jerked upright, obviously uncomfortable. "I'm not permitted to talk about that one."

It just made her want to know about it all the more. "Oh, come on, Eugene. Why do you get to know everything? Let me see."

"No!" he barked. He had never been that abrupt with her before. He must have realized how he sounded, because he composed himself and went on more quietly. "I mean, we can't. Mr. Whittaker was adamant that this program be left alone. It is not to be touched under any circumstances."

Oh no. She wasn't going to let him get away with *that*. "It couldn't hurt to have a quick peek."

He took several short breaths. Was he hyperventilating?

"Miss Kendall, we're not communicating very well

this evening. First, Mr. Whittaker didn't want you to know this computer and room even exist—and now you know. Second, Mr. Whittaker doesn't want you to touch the Applesauce program—and now you're trying to persuade me to go against his wishes." His face was very red. "I won't do it! And I'm extremely disappointed that you're persisting. I expected better behavior from you."

She suddenly realized he was serious. She felt bad that she had brought him to this point. She held up her hands in surrender and tried to make light of the situation. "All right, all right! You don't have to get all preachy with me! It's just a computer program. I didn't think it was such a big deal." She laid a hand on his arm. "I'm sorry, okay?"

His breathing became more measured, and his face slowly returned to its normal color. "Apology accepted. Now I must insist that we leave . . . immediately. Mabel, log off."

"Logging off." *Beep, whir, blink.* "Good-bye."

CHAPTER THIRTEEN

The next morning was Connie's turn to open the shop. Eugene had a study group at the college and would be in a little later. Whit called soon after she opened and said he would be in that afternoon. As usual on a Saturday, the place soon filled up with kids. She was just finishing setting up the soda counter when Donna Barclay walked up.

"Connie."

"Hi, Donna. Feeling better today?"

Donna shrugged. "Sort of."

"Sort of? Did you see Richard Maxwell again?"

"No, but I have a feeling I might."

"Why?"

Donna sighed. "I haven't talked to Mr. Whittaker yet about what happened yesterday. You know how he is about these things. He'll want me to go back and visit Mrs. Hooper again."

Connie nodded sympathetically. "That sounds like Whit, all right. But you know why he'll want you to do that, don't you?"

Donna rolled her eyes. "Yeah. Because it's the right thing to do."

Connie smiled. "And not just for Mrs. Hooper, but for *you*."

"You know, *that* sounds like Mr. Whittaker too," Donna said, grinning. "Anyway, I thought before I talked with him, I'd have a little fun with the train set. But it isn't working, and I can't find the switch to turn it on."

Connie thought for a second, then remembered. "Oh, that's right. Eugene turned it off at the computer last night."

Donna looked confused. "Huh?"

"Nothing. I'll get the train running for you, but I need to go to the office for a few minutes. Can you watch the soda counter for me, Donna? Just let me know if a customer comes in."

"Sure!"

Connie rounded the counter's corner, crossed the room, and bounded up the stairs. She had a set of keys on a lanyard around her neck, and when she got to the office door, she sorted through them, selected the right one, unlocked the door, and walked inside.

She tried to remember what Eugene did when they left last evening. First, she needed to get the bookcase out of the way. Eugene locked it—the keyhole was in the wall next to the case. Now where did he put the key? Yes . . . in one of the books. But which one? She searched the books, trying to recall. The titles flipped by: *Voyage of the Dawn Treader*, *The Magician's Nephew*,

The Silver Chair. Wait! This one. This was it. *The Last Battle*.

She took the book from the shelf and opened it. Sure enough, the key was pressed inside the front cover. She retrieved the key, set down the book, inserted the key in the lock, and turned it. There was a loud click and a soft, vacuum-like sound. The bookcase creaked as it slowly swung open. The familiar hum of the computer greeted her.

She stepped into the room and up to the big screen. Now how did she get this thing to work? Maybe if she just talked to it like Eugene did. She cleared her throat and adopted a serious tone. "Mabel?"

Beep. Whir. "Good morning, John Avery Whittaker."

So much for serious. She giggled. "It's not him. I mean, I'm me. I mean, I'm not John Avery Whittaker. I'm Connie. Why am I explaining this to a stupid computer?" A breath. "Mabel, I need you to turn on the trains, please."

Beep. "I do not understand."

She frowned. Weren't computers supposed to be smart? She slowed down and spoke louder. "Turn. On. The. Trains. You know, trains? Wooo-wooo! Tracks? Chugga-chugga-chugga? Turn them on."

Beep, whir. "Please make your selection from the program menu."

Connie blinked. "Oh! Good idea. The program menu; that's what Eugene said." The menu appeared on the big screen. She scanned it and found "train-set program." Now how did Eugene say it again? "Mabel, please, uh, please . . . oh yeah! Please load the train-set program."

Beep. "Loading train-set program."

Ha! Success. All right!

Beep-beep. "Train-set program loaded. Run train-set program?"

"Uh, yes, Mabel. Run train-set program."

Beep-beep. "Train-set program is running."

Connie grinned broadly. "Great! Thanks. Boy, this is so easy. Eugene isn't the only brainy one, Councilman Glossman."

Beep, whir. "Please make your next selection from the program menu."

"Next selection? I don't want to make a next sel—"

She stopped. There it was on the menu screen.

Applesauce.

Curiosity suddenly overwhelmed her. She wondered what Whit put in the program. Maybe it was a file about her. One of those personnel files about how she was doing. No, Whit would tell her if she was doing something wrong. Wouldn't he?

Her brow furrowed. What if he hadn't been happy about her work and didn't have the heart to tell her? If the file was about her, she should be allowed to see it, shouldn't she?

"I'll bet Eugene's looked at it," she muttered. It wasn't fair. Why should he get to know all the secrets, especially ones about her? She didn't get to know any of *his* secrets. Maybe they were in the file too.

Yeah, that *must* be it! Both of their files were on there, and now she'd be able to see his secrets like he'd seen hers. A little peek wouldn't make any difference—not if she and Eugene were truly equals. She cleared her throat again. "Ah, Mabel? Please load the program called—"

"Connie?"

She jumped and shrieked. "Aaah! *What?*"

It was Donna standing frozen and wide eyed in the computer-room doorway. "Wow. I didn't mean to scare you!"

Beep, whir, boop. "Please repeat command. I do not have a program called Aaah-what."

Donna stepped into the room. "Look at all this equipment!"

Connie's heart raced. "No. You don't see this, Donna. Promise me you don't see it. Just go back to the counter and forget about it. Promise me, okay?"

Donna backed away, looking at Connie as if she was crazy. "Uh, sure, okay, whatever you say, Connie. I've just never seen—"

"I know, I know. I said the same thing when I saw

it." She forced herself to calm down. "But you have to pretend like you *didn't* see it. Nobody's supposed to know it's here. Okay? Please?"

Donna still looked wary but nodded. "Okay. I didn't see it. It doesn't exist."

"Thanks. I'll be out in a minute."

"Okay." Donna turned and walked away, shaking her head and muttering, "Wow."

Connie exhaled, relieved. She couldn't believe what she almost did.

Beep. "Please repeat command."

She turned back to the screen. "No, just forget it, Mabel."

Beep. "I do not understand."

"I wanted you to load Applesauce, but—"

Beep, whir. "Loading Applesauce."

"What? No. Don't!"

Beep. "Applesauce is loaded. Please push any key to continue."

"But I don't want to push a key."

Whir. "Push any key to continue."

"I told you—"

Whir. "Push any key to continue."

Connie growled. "All right, all right!" She punched the space bar as though it were a red-hot coal. "There. I've pushed the key. Now will you just stop and—"

Beep, whir, beep. "Applesauce level one. Internal matrix for Whit's End is loaded. Systems check beginning."

Her eyes widened. "Internal *what?* Mabel, what are you doing?"

The computer beeped, whirred, and blinked faster and faster. And now there were other noises as well. They were outside the room but within the building: clanking, honking, buzzing, ringing, whirring, knocking, pinging, revving, and a muffled alarm. Connie looked back and forth rapidly between the noises out there and the beeping, whirring, and blinking in the room.

"What's all the noise? What are you doing, Mabel?"

Donna ran back into the room, looking scared. "Connie! Connie! Everything's going crazy—all the displays, the trains, the Imagination Station. They're going nuts!"

Connie's heart pounded and she started to sweat. She whipped around to the screen. "Oh no oh no oh no. Don't do this to me, please. I'm sorry! How do I turn this thing off?" She started mashing keys on the computer keyboard. "One of these has to turn it off!"

Donna pointed to the ESC key. "Try that one!"

Connie pressed it repeatedly. "I am, I am! Just go and tell everyone to . . . to get out of the building. Pretend it's a fire drill or something. And *be calm*!"

"Okay, Connie!" Donna ran out of the office. The noises in the building got louder and more frenzied. What was the stupid computer doing? And why was it doing this to her? She yelled, "*Heeeeellllllp!*"

Suddenly Eugene was at the computer-room door. "Miss Kendall! What's going on here? The entire facility is—"

She grabbed his arm and pulled him into the room. "Eugene! Am I glad to see you. You have to stop this thing. *Please*. I'll never touch it again, I promise. But *please* make it stop."

His eyes scanned the big screen. "What did you do?" His jaw dropped. He looked horrified. "Applesauce. You loaded Applesauce!"

She was near tears now. "It was an accident. I didn't mean to. Just stop it."

He brushed her aside and said in a commanding voice, "Mabel. Do you hear me? Please respond, Mabel!"

Beepboopboopbeep. Beepboopboopbeep. "Systems check nearing completion."

"But, *Mabel*—"

Beepwhirwhirboopbeep. "Systems check finalizing."

"Mabel, discontinue—"

Beepbeepboopboop. "Systems check complete."

Almost instantly, all noises wound down. Mabel's beeping, booping, whirring, and blinking decreased.

After a few seconds, Whit's End seemed to return to normal. All Connie could hear was her heart pounding in her ears, and her and Eugene's heavy breaths. She touched him on the arm. "It stopped. You made it stop."

He looked at the big screen warily. "I'm not sure I did anything."

She exhaled sharply. "I don't care. It stopped. Oh, Whit's going to kill me!"

Eugene still faced the screen but spoke to Connie very carefully. "Well, dare I say it? If we close up this room and go about our business, Mr. Whittaker need never know."

She was touched. "Eugene . . . would you do that for me?"

He shook his head. "Not just for you; for both of us. Now let's get out of—"

Beep, whir, beep. "Applesauce proceeding to level two."

Eugene gulped. "Level . . . two?"

Connie's heart started pounding again. "What does that mean, level two?"

"I don't know."

Whir. "Please enter password."

His shoulders drooped. "She wants a password."

Whir. "Please enter password."

Eugene held up his hands. "I don't know the password."

Connie whacked him on the shoulder. "Make something up."

Whir, beep. "You have ten seconds to enter password."

A different beeping started, deeper and evenly paced. It grew steadily louder with each beep, and as it did, the noises around Whit's End wound up again and increased.

Connie was getting frantic. "Everything's going nuts again! What's it doing?"

Eugene shook his head. "I don't know, but I need a password!"

Beep. "Ten."

"Uh . . . applesauce," Eugene guessed.

Beep. "Nine."

"Whit's End! John Avery!"

Connie grabbed Eugene's shirt. "What will it do?"

Beep. "Eight."

"Tom Riley! Whittaker!"

Beep. "Seven."

"Eugene, what's it—"

"Quiet, Miss Kendall! Bible!"

Beep. "Six."

Eugene shouted. "His wife's name?"

Beep. "Five."

"What was it?" he squeaked.

Beep. "Four."

Connie drew a complete blank. "Uh . . ."

Beep. "Three."

Eugene's face was red. "Connie?"

Beep. "Two."

"I don't remember!"

Beep. "One. You have failed to provide a password. System will now shut down functions until further information is supplied."

In the soda shop and events rooms, the displays and machines ran at a fever pace, the noises combining into a cacophony. Mabel's beeps, boops, and whirs increased rapidly, and her lights blinked so fast, they began to strobe. Connie covered her ears. Eugene grimaced. Mabel's voice slowed down. "Have . . . a . . . nice . . . daaaaay."

The activity peaked. There were electrical surges, the room lights flickered, there was a loud snap, and then everything suddenly turned off. It wasn't just the rooms and Mabel but the overhead lights, air-conditioning, outside lights, and everything that made the place run. It all flashed, ground to a halt, and went silent and dark. The whole building was completely quiet, completely dead.

Eugene's breathing was very shallow. He whispered, "Oh no."

Connie pulled on his T-shirt sleeve. Her voice quavered. "Eugene? What happened? What have we done?"

He looked extremely pale. "I think . . . we killed Whit's End."

❖

A few moments later, many miles away, a soft ding announced the arrival of a notice on a computer screen. The notice read, simply, "Applesauce engaged. Level one successful. Level-two security measures successful. Total shutdown achieved."

The owner of the screen leaned back in his chair, smiled, and growled softly, "Excellent." He pressed an autodial button on his phone and then pushed the speaker button.

After three rings, the phone clicked, and a filtered voice on the other end said, "Glossman."

"Hello, Philip. Have you found him yet?"

"Yes. He's working as an orderly at the retirement

home. You can pretty much guess what he's doing there."

"Mmm. Petty but useful. Pick him up and bring him to me."

"To you? In Chicago?"

"Was I unclear?"

"N-no, sir, but I-I thought you wanted me to put him to work disrupting things here in Odyssey—"

"Events have accelerated, Philip. I take it you talked to Whittaker's employees as I asked you to?"

"Yes, sir, one of them anyway. The girl—Connie."

"Mmm. Well, whatever you said to her has worked out splendidly. So I'll need Maxwell's skills sooner than expected. Which is why I must meet with him face-to-face. Bring him. Now."

"Yes, sir."

"Have you found a building for Webster Development yet?"

"Yes, sir. We're already putting measures in place to acquire it."

He smiled. "Excellent."

CHAPTER FOURTEEN

All Connie and Eugene could do was wait. She went out to the front porch where the kids were gathered and sent them home. There was nothing for them there, nothing to do now, nothing they could play with, examine, explore, or experience. She couldn't even fix them a sundae or other treat.

Once they were gone, she came back inside and sat

in a booth at the far corner of the soda fountain. After a bit, Eugene came downstairs, saw where she was, and sat down opposite her. Neither of them spoke.

Later (was it minutes or hours?), the front door opened and the bell above the door tinkled. In the absolute quiet, it sounded like an explosion and a gong, followed by footsteps that boomed like cannons with each step. Every noise echoed with a genuine hollowness. The footsteps rounded the entryway into the soda fountain and stopped.

John Avery Whittaker had returned.

"What's all this?" he muttered. Then he called out, "Connie? Eugene?"

She didn't want to let him know where they were, but Eugene coughed softly. "Over here, Mr. Whittaker."

Whit approached them. "Why is everything so dark? Where are all the kids?"

Connie felt sick, as though she'd throw up if she opened her mouth.

Eugene answered again, shakily. "W-we felt it was best to send the young patrons home."

Whit frowned. "But why? What happened?"

Connie finally found her voice and blurted out, "It all shut down. Everything!"

"Everything?" He looked back and forth at each of them. "Will you please tell me what happened?"

Connie looked at Eugene; he looked at her. Neither spoke. Whit let out a frustrated sigh. "Well?"

She tried to smile. "Do you wanna guess?"

"No!"

She went silent again.

Whit scowled. "This is silly. You're both adults. Now tell me what happened."

She cleared her throat and took a deep breath. "Eugene didn't know the password."

Eugene gave her a startled look. "Now just a moment—"

Whit cut in. "The password?" His face fell. "Not for Applesauce!"

Connie and Eugene exchanged guilty glances, and then both turned back to Whit, eyes down, and nodded.

Whit's shoulders drooped. He looked genuinely grieved. "Oh no. No."

He looked so sad, so disappointed. Connie couldn't bear for him to be upset with her. "It's not my fault, Whit! Not all of it. See, I had to turn on the train because Eugene turned it off last night, and I accidentally loaded Applesauce, and everything started going crazy, and I panicked and Eugene came and—" She had to stop.

Whit looked at her with a piercing stare.

She deflated. Her voice was tiny. "This . . . doesn't sound very good, does it?"

"How did you know the computer was there, Connie?"

She looked down. "Well, ah, Eugene?"

Whit shifted his stare to Eugene, who cleared his throat uncomfortably. "I-I should have locked the office door, Mr. Whittaker. I should have been more careful. The train wouldn't turn off, so I went into the computer room, and Miss Kendall saw me and—" He swallowed hard. "This whole thing sounds rather ridiculous, doesn't it?" He smiled weakly.

But Whit didn't smile back. His expression was stern. "No, not at all. In fact, it's extremely serious."

Connie looked at him searchingly. "But you can fix everything, right, Whit? You can make everything right again, can't you?"

"I can try," he said evenly. "But it won't be easy. You see, Applesauce has a purpose that goes far beyond just Whit's End. It was designed for many other things that I can't tell you about. That's why I installed a fail-safe system."

"Fail-safe?"

Eugene piped in. "A system that shuts everything down if an unidentified user tries to break in."

Whit nodded. "You didn't know the password, so Mabel figured you didn't belong there. She was right."

Eugene lowered his head. "I should have known."

Connie took another deep breath and braced herself. "Okay, Whit . . . go ahead. We deserve it."

Whit looked confused. "Deserve what?"

"The lecture. We let you down. Go on. Rip into us. We're ready."

His stare pierced her soul. "You don't seem to understand, Connie. I-I can't simply lecture you. There is more at stake here than that." He sank into a chair and sighed deeply. He looked so sad, she thought he might be sick.

She reached out to him. "Whit, what's wrong?"

"I trusted you. I trusted you both to respect my wishes. You—Eugene—to keep that computer room a secret and stay away from Applesauce. And you—Connie—to curb your curiosity enough to know that if I had something to share with you, I would. I trusted you. That trust has been broken."

She was near tears. "I'm sorry, Whit. I really, truly am."

Eugene put his hand to his chest. "As am I, Mr. Whittaker!"

Whit nodded slowly. "I believe you. But this time,

sorry isn't enough. You both breached my trust in a very serious way."

Connie didn't like where this was going at all. She put her hands on his arm. "We'll make it up to you. We'll do anything!"

Whit looked down, and when he looked up again, his piercing stare was gone, but his eyes were filled with tears. "I'm sorry. This grieves me. But I have no choice."

Connie looked from Whit to Eugene. All the blood had drained from Eugene's face. He was so pale, he looked like a ghost. He opened and closed his mouth several times, but no sound came out. Tears were now streaming down Connie's cheeks. This couldn't be happening! Whit wouldn't do it. How could he do it? Couldn't he see how anguished they were, how truly remorseful? She was certain he could. But incredibly, unbelievably, it wasn't going to matter.

Whit stood and breathed in deeply. "Eugene. Connie. Because of what you've done today, effective immediately you are no longer employees of Whit's End." A tear escaped from the corner of his eye and trickled down his face. "You're both . . . fired."

No! "Whit," Connie pleaded softly.

"If you'll excuse me, I have some cleaning up to do." He turned, walked away from them, mounted the stairs, and was gone.

Eugene sniffled miserably.

Connie wept bitterly. "Whit."

✙

Keep reading for a preview of book 2, *Pawn's Play*.

BOOK 2 PREVIEW

Richard Maxwell was sweating.

A lot.

Despite the cool air of his present location—wherever it was—sweat beaded on his forehead and upper lip and trickled down his back, soaking his shirt. He had obviously messed up somewhere. But how? He was certain he had accounted for all the variables. No one could have known. He didn't make any mistakes.

Or so he thought until a few hours ago. That's when he realized how wrong he was.

Was it a few hours ago? It could have been longer. It was hard to tell time in the back of a sealed-up van with no windows or lights.

It was like something out of a bad movie: he was walking home from his job at the retirement home, having just pulled off his best haul yet, when a van pulled up beside him, and two beefy guys manhandled him into the back. They slid the door shut, and the van took off so fast, he slid to the rear and banged his head against the back door.

They drove for a long time, and when they finally stopped and opened the door, he was surprised to see they were in a nearly empty warehouse. The only things in it were the van and a small table with two chairs lit by a pool of light from the ceiling. The beefy guys pulled him out of the van and sat him down in one of the chairs. One of them placed the backpack of pilfered items on the table, and then they both turned and left, their footsteps echoing in the darkness.

✛

A man with pasty skin, thinning salt-and-pepper hair, a potbelly, and milky gray eyes sat in the chair opposite him, looking at the contents of a file folder. The angle of the light caused his hooked nose to cast a strange shadow across his mouth and chin.

Without looking up, the man said, "Richard Maxwell: con artist, swindler, manipulator, and now—" He set down the folder and upended the backpack. The day's haul spilled onto the table. The man smirked at him. "—petty thief. My, my, you've led quite a life for someone so young, haven't you?"

Richard thought there was something familiar about this guy. He'd seen him somewhere. It hit him. "I know you. You're like a city-government guy from Odyssey, right?"

The man smiled a greasy sort of smile. "Not *like*. *Am*. Councilman Philip Glossman. I wish I could say I was pleased to make your acquaintance. But I'm not."

Richard licked his lips nervously. "Look, I was just holding that stuff for a friend—"

Glossman held up a finger and wagged it, pursing his lips and shaking his head slightly. "Please. Don't even try."

This was weird, Richard thought. Since when could city councilmen arrest people? And why all the subterfuge? He fought to stay cool. "So where am I? What is this place?"

"All in good time, Richard. All in good time." Glossman examined the contents of the backpack. He picked up a gold brooch shaped like a butterfly. Tiny, sparkling diamonds lined its wings. "Pretty," he smirked. "Though it doesn't really go with your outfit."

That was it. Richard slammed his hands on the table and jumped up. "What is this? What's going on here?"

Glossman continued smirking. "Sit down, Richard," he said evenly.

Richard leaned across the table. "I've got rights! You can't arrest me without telling me why."

Glossman laughed. "Who said you're arrested?"

Richard leaned back slowly and swallowed hard. "If you're not arresting me, then . . ." He sank down in the chair, heart pounding. "You're kidnapping me?"

A bigger laugh. "Hardly! Why kidnap someone nobody would pay a ransom for?"

"Then what's going on?" His voice was almost pleading. "Why did you bring me here?"

Glossman scooted back his chair, stood, and stepped behind it. "I've brought you here to meet someone—someone who very much wants to meet you." He turned his head and called into the darkness behind him. "Sir!"

Richard heard a door open, though he saw no light. The door closed. One set of footsteps accompanied by the occasional tap-tap of a walking stick echoed in the empty building. They were headed right toward him and grew louder with each step and tap.

Suddenly a man appeared in the pool of light. He was tall and lean with angular features. He wore a black, three-piece suit, tailored to fit him perfectly. The coat fell almost to his knees, the trousers were sharply creased, and his black shoes were polished to a high gloss. He carried a black walking stick with a polished gold knob for a handle. His hair was jet black, save for white streaks that ran from both temples to the back of his head. His mustache and Vandyke beard were also jet black.

Glossman held out the chair for the man, and he glided into it with an easy grace, placing his walking stick on the table atop the pilfered loot. He looked across the table and smiled, teeth gleaming, and his gaze sent chills down Richard's spine.

"Hello, Richard." The man's voice was deep, dark, rich, and cold as ice. "I'm Dr. Regis Blackgaard. You and I need to talk."